In Cofeina Veritas!

In Coffee Lies the Truth

Cristian Neagu

authorHOUSE®

AuthorHouse™
1663 Liberty Drive
Bloomington, IN 47403
www.authorhouse.com
Phone: 1-800-839-8640

Published by AuthorHouse   8/20/12

ISBN: 978-1-4772-2211-9 (sc)
ISBN: 978-1-4772-2212-6 (dj)
ISBN: 978-1-4772-2213-3 (e)

"Insane, but not irresponsible"

To my father.

Acknowledgements

First and foremost I want to thank Farhad and Ali from The Courtyard Brasserie, for their trust and support. Without them, my dream would have never turned into reality.

I want to dedicate this book to my brother Daniel for being beside me since our father passed away.

Also many thanks:

To Michael Reeds for his professional advices and guidance.

To Madalina, for being 'The One' and to her parents, Dorina and Ioan Sava for their love and care. I will always cherish the time spent together.

To Mihai Moraru for the endless nights when he shared his wisdom and wine.

To Stefania Petra and her twisted mind for giving me a glimpse of happiness.

To Ghita Bizau for adding life in every chapter with his drawings.

To Martin Ceklovsky for his advices, his patience and for being there to calm me down every time I panicked.

To the people whom discovered 'chaoua', widely known as 'coffee'

And to all those that, at least once in their lives sat with me for a coffee.

"Bang" Log
Instead of a preface

"Your head is filled with rainbows, coffee, and fries, with savory and crazy ideas!" she says in the middle of our discussion about "the beginning." I wanted to inoculate the idea of "majestic," "grandiose" on her. All important things have such a beginning. And all have gone "bang."

"Bang!" and there's the universe! "Bang!" and a child is born. "Bang!" goes the champagne, and everyone is ecstatic. "Bang!" and the cucumber jar is open. (Be careful; if the jar doesn't go "bang," it means it was not sealed and it's possible that the product inside has been tainted!)

But! There is, as expected, a something. I am not majestic, grandiose, etc. I am Dan, and I don't even go "bang," even if this is my beginning. I do things that, in my mind, have the role of cleaning the world of infections. I'm no doctor, just a detective, and my role is investigating and solving (preferably with a positive result) cases of crime, regardless of their nature or importance. Don't be scared, you won't see me on the streets, running like a lunatic or tearing down your door because I suspect that you are guilty of witchcraft or who knows of what other types of accusations you'll find in my books. This is all happening in my world, which you consider fiction. (The same thing I can say about you, reader!)

There's not much to say about the author. I've chosen him because, despite his proven stubbornness and impulsiveness, he has ten fingers in perfect harmony with his mind. He's a human paradox. He doesn't need much time to pass from a true contagious source of happiness to an absent fetus, lost in the infinity of thoughts. But we're working on the same frequency, and many times he left me with the impression that he knows what I'm about to do, without me giving him any clue. That's a mystery I'll undertake when he loses his inoffensiveness. Besides that, he has humor and patience (which he loses rather quickly, so he doesn't have it. Typical to him).

Others? Yes, there are "others" who have gone ahead of you. Most of them were curious, only a part of them were anxious, and only few have shared their opinions.

"I finished reading your book ... actually, since last night ... I wasn't patient to read it as I planned, a few pages last night, a few today ... tomorrow. You have reminded me why I loved spending entire nights reading books! Your story manages to maintain the reader's attention alert, the fine humor with which it's exposed, small self-ironies here and there, and even the aggressivity of Dan Demetriad give it a certain charm. You have offered me an interesting reading, and I will, most definitely, read it again, at leisure!

Cristina

"With a style overflowing with vitality and humor, ironic and intelligent, Cristian Neagu brings you in the world of the phlegmatic detective Dan Demetriad, without realizing that, in fact, it's not you in there."

Let's Not Chatter

"You've got talent! Yes, the reality is that you've got a 'hand' for this."

Stage Director

"Full of phlegmatic and ironic humor, resembling the style of Vlad Musatescu ... I love this writer. I like your attention to details, your suggestive description of characters, the use of flashbacks.

Weird self-description in the beginning, but, eventually, you are both weird."

Geta Chitu

"When are you publishing it? I want one, definitely. Yes, it's fully worth it! It has the greatest detective in all detective novels I have read, but it drives me crazy that I always thought it's obvious who the murderer is, I just couldn't find the connection."

Cora Radu

And you? Well, you've made the first step. However, I recommend a comfortable position, a large cup of coffee, and let me tell you what it's all about …

Chapter I

Or the first

I hate the sun in the morning … it's like it's slapping me dearly, just to ruin my good mood. I throw my feet out of bed and hide my head between my hands so I can steal a few more seconds of sleep. It's been forever. With a little effort, I get up and slowly go toward the kitchen, where my espresso machine awaits. This technological engineering I seized more than two years ago, from a gang of lunatics. I was walking quietly on the street in the evening so I can maintain my fitness before my glass of warm milk, intended for easing my sleep. All right, it wasn't really evening—it was almost morning, and I wasn't walking for maintaining my fitness, but I was returning from Alex, a girl I have committed myself to quite a lot during those few hours spent in town, but one can say that that evening I worked my every muscle with her. At least the glass of warm milk existed! Warm milk, coffee, and a drop of sugar. And hurrying to drink it, I see those lunatics running while holding the espresso machine. I was never curious where they had gotten it from, but the fact that they were running and holding it made me think, so I chased them down and I seized it. They had "borrowed" it from the former workplace of one of them, rationalizing that the company still owed him a tranche of money. That mattered too little, and the important thing is that everyone was happy, them because they did not end up in court, and I because I changed the kettle. And now it's dear to me, and not a day goes by that I don't put it to work. The big red button works wonders. I just push it and I hear how that engineering starts planting, watering, cropping, roasting, and grinding the coffee. Actually, this is all in my imagination, but at least it spares me of an extra job. I sit down quietly at my laptop's keyboard, in the steams of coffee, and search for the tobacco like heck. I know it's on the desk somewhere, but it's very difficult to see it with just one open eye. I reconcile, and I wait to wake up.

I read the media, and the society news shocks me. I totally lack interest, but at least I have something to match my coffee with. My thoughts are shattered by an irritating sound coming from the hall table. Yes, it's another technical engineering, which is striking my synapses each time. I pick up the phone and I suavely answer with my rasped and irritated voice.

"Yes ... for the moment I am not here, so leave the beep after the message ... no, the other way around ..."

"Hello, Mihai Badea here, am I disturbing?"

"All due respect, I can tell you that you have already did, but since I am already here ... what's it about?"

"I apologize, it's about a dog, specifically, my dog ... it's been missing for a few days and we can't manage to find it. It's like it melted into thin air."

"Mister Badea, don't get me wrong, but the only missing animals I search for are humans. Dogs are taken care of by the veterinarian—the flayer, not the officer—do you understand me?"

"I know, but someone recommended you as a first-class detective, and that dog was very important for us."

"Don't tell me, it buys your groceries and cleans your house?"

"No, sir, he was part of the family."

"You know that you can be accused of zoophilia for this statement, don't you?"

"Sir, I'm being serious."

"That's exactly what I was afraid of!"

"However, let's be reasonable and discuss concretely. Name a price!"

"It's nine in the morning. I don't think so early. I'm sorry for your dog, but I'm really not going to ferret among bushes for a mutt who has instinctively left to unload hormones with some bitch in heat, so have a nice day!"

I throw the receiver in the cradle, hoping to break it and to make it quiet for good.

I don't manage to turn on my heels when that rrring raises my arm hair.

"I'm sorry, I'm really not going to undertake your ca—"

"Boss, good morning. Can you come to the station. We received an emergency phone call."

I am Chief Quaestor at the forensics department, and I also do some detective work in private, for those who don't want to be associated with the police. The man on the phone is my right hand. More of left, and rather a foot, at least a toe, Cezar, young graduate of the Academy and with some interventions from his father, senator on the job, and an influential person in his spare time, I took him under my wing. Maybe I can get some results from this package of imbecility. He's got a certain something that intrigues me and makes me curious.

"Cezar, I'll be right there—after I have my coffee, that is."

I was still hoping that I could spend this week licking my wounds and vegging, but it seems the world is too agitated nowadays. I have my coffee on the run, while dressing in a shirt, ironed in a hurry, only on the chest because I'll have my coat over it anyway and nobody will notice, and then I leave hastily, walking toward the headquarters, which is just a few blocks away. Anyway, I think my "booth" with wheels already got to the scrap yard, after the stupid accident in which a well-boozed and death-wishing concreter decided not to check twice while backing his sixteen-ton concrete mixer. My luck was that it was not loaded; otherwise, it would have turned my former car in a superb monument.

I get there, and everyone greets politely, a part of them with great efforts. I answer blank and I head for the office, where Cezar minds his business. He minds my business, again playing on the computer because "yours shows images better than mine." Well, of course, when you have funds at hand, you aim the highest you can.

"Tell me, kid, what's the status?"

"Two dead persons found in a house at the edge of the city. Police are already on the scene, but they want someone from forensics."

"Ugly day they've chosen to die. Grab your notebook and a pen and let's go."

We get there at a little over ten. The place is crowded with policemen, some busy, some with coffee, pictures, and yellow tape circling the area. We're in the outskirts of the town, in a not so desirable neighborhood. Houses here look like they are deserted for some time but you would be amazed to find out how many people can fit into a single bedroom house! Well, without outskirts there would be no city center. And without criminals I would be out of job.

It's a neighborhood of ill repute, and it seems the two murders do not affect the neighbors one bit. One of the victims was found hanging by the ceiling like a stuffed teddy bear on the review mirror, and the other one was lying down in a pool of blood. The hypothesis of the police is that one of them tied himself to the chandelier and the other one, coming home and finding his friend hanging, put a bullet through his brain. An interesting, simple and comfortable, but at the same time wrong idea! How much of a friend can you be of someone if you blow your brains when seeing the other one dangling adrift? Looking more closely around their hands, they both had scratch marks and bruises, and the one hanging had on his neck two sets of marks, the latter ones being left by the rope, and, according their color, appearing post-mortem. Also, looking at them you can say that the last thing filling their stomach was air. Later on, this detail was confirmed by the autopsy, its report showing that the persons were, if I may say so, dead with hunger. The problem was another. In the house, I had seen dirty dishes and food cooked at least a day before, and in the waste basket I found two shopping receipts from the day before from a local supermarket. My hypothesis is the following.

The individuals, subsequently confirmed to have been members of a gang handling the distribution of exhilaration pills and cigars, had old debts, which they could not pay. The recuperators came to visit and have not hurried, but stayed there for a few days, trying to make the best of those two, insisting, apparently, on their souls. Seeing that they were not successful, they devised the idea of a double suicide. The manner of working shows they're not too smart and are mostly used with raw force.

The same day, I went shopping in the same place, it seemed they had really good deals for coffee. As expected, the video cameras were focused on the cash registers. An ID pulled out of the pocket resulted in a CD from the computer with the footage of the previous day. Having the hour, date, and number of the cash register marked on the receipt, I have managed to identify an "unidentified person" shopping for daily groceries.

"How selfish, Cezar. Look at him. A bag of milk, a wheel of cheese, one salami, two chops."

4

"What's wrong, boss? He must've been hungry."

"Yes, Cezar, but what were the other two ingesting, flies and limestone?"

The face on the tape was already in our database, so he was identified within twenty-four hours. It wasn't too hard to find out where we can find him. And look at me standing against the miserable's wall. I was the most normally dressed. A life jacket, not for sailors but for policemen, pulled my shirt against my body. I also had a fashionable helmet with a visor over my face and chin, useful just I case I got spat on. An assault with any contusive object would have shattered it. I, a nice guy, knock on the door. The others, nice guys, knock the door down. With a ram. The door collapses loudly, like in the movies, also tearing the frame and pieces of the wall. The joyful guys, Or who accompanied me, dressed like androids you could gather with a magnet, break in yelling with all their love available, each with their own "police, get on the ground"; "mother, I love you"; or "hey, my wife's pregnant." Honestly, the words didn't matter, but the effect did. Triumphant, I finally enter, adopting the position of a great battalion commander coming to reap. I find the murderer, who has now become the victim, moaning under the weight of the androids standing on top of him like in elementary school, when we were jumping on "gramada cere varf."[1]

"Hey, guys, if you won't get down from on top of him, I cannot identify him."

"Sir, what if he has a gun?"

"Well, if he had a gun, we would be lesser by minimum one. And I don't think he can hide a Kalashnikov in his underwear. Come on, get him up."

Said and done, in a few seconds they were standing with the guy tightly held by all limbs. He looked as full of energy as a fresh cucumber.

"Chief Quaestor Dan Demetriad at your service. How may I be of assistance?"

The individual stares at me greatly and surprised, but his eyes gave him away. He knows exactly why we are here.

"My apologies," I continue. "Dan Demetriad. What is your name?"

---

1 "Gramada cere varf" – "the pile requires a peak" game usually played by youngsters, in which one of them stumbles or is thrown to the ground, and the others pile up on top of him.

Nothing.

"Me earthling, you who?"

Nothing.

"You, sturgeon, are finished anyway, but I'll penalize your every relative only for existing if you don't start talking! And plus, I'll stick toothpicks under your nails."

"What do you want from me. Do you have a warrant?"

"We have a warrant, we have evidence, we have bodies, we have time."

"What evidence, what bodies?"

I remove my helmet and hit him loudly in the face. The guys look at me and nod, confirming that this kind of accident happens during descents.

"Let's be civilized and not waste our time around here. If you won't speak now, you will speak downtown, and please be advised that Preda, our questioning guy, is upset because his wife cheated on him, and it's very likely that he will blow off steam on you before he even asks you something."

Bang. Again. The helmet is very rigid and quite durable. I'm polishing it on the individual's face until blood floods his mouth and nose.

"Demetriad, Demetriad Dan," he babbles through blood bubbles.

"In person. And you?"

"Metea Costin. Demetriad Dan."

"You cannot be both, because one of them is me. Come on, guys, wrap him nicely, get on your horses, and go to headquarters."

The recent crimes he described in detail, from the first step he made in the infelicitous' house, until the last push on the door handle on his way out. Preda also made him tell how, as a child, he stole a neighbor's toy. He even gave us the name of his accomplice, a well known character from another city, whom my colleagues have managed to take into custody the very next day. He was minding his daily routine without even considering that he could be uncovered. Preda also managed to obtain other information from him, useful for the police. Even more, our guy got back together with his wife, it seems he forgave her. Something helped him discharge, but nobody knows what. And, go figure, my hypothesis sounds like I had witnessed what happened. Another short and bubbly success, just like vitamins in a glass.

Another morning, the same apartment, another coffee, the same telephone.

"Yes, please!"

"Boss, it's me, Cezar. We have received a homonymous call at the station about a kidnapping."

"Anonymous, Cezar, anonymous."

"Right. Can you come? I think it's important."

I'm living a déjà vu. I am in no way excited about the situation and, even more, the heat outside turns me into a real spring, flooding the shirt hidden under my coat. But I cannot leave without it, because I would look like used toilet paper. Sometimes, I totally lack any interest in the way I'm dressed. The articles of clothing covering my nudity don't excite me one bit. I just love the tribes where they have only one robe, a bunch of reeds wrapped around the crotch. Unfortunately, society would classify me as being stuck somewhere on the evolutionary scale between a chimpanzee and a quince if I were to adopt that costume, and I don't even want to begin to think about the rash caused by that particular theca. So I conform, not without militating for naturalness with every opportunity occurred, especially for the feminine one.

I reach the headquarters. I sneak through people to my office, deliberately ignoring all greetings and congratulations from my coworkers. After all this time, they still haven't got used to the fact that I don't care. There, Cezar serves me at the entrance with a large feed of information.

"Boss, the anonymous called earlier and he said that he has the son of … let me look it up, I wrote down what he said … yes, here!" He slips under my eyes a piece of paper where several short sentences were written in an intelligible manner.

"Today we picked up Marius Badea from the train station in Craiova. You will also receive confirmation that we have it, as well as details on the ransom. It is recommended that you cooperate in order to avoid any inconvenience."

"Good … so far, we only have a 'homonymous' information. Tell me something about this lad. I suppose you have already done some research."

"Well, boss, I searched a bit, and here it says that he's the son of Mihai Badea, owner of some night clubs in Craiova, and he also owns

7

shares at some oil platfonts in the Persian Gulf, which he sells directly to the large fuel manufacturers in Europe."

"Platforms, kid, platforms. Interesting but senseless ... In the first phase, it seems like a classic job. The man has money. Others don't have but want it, and look at the solution they've found."

"I'll go notify the colleagues. Let's see who might help us with this investigation."

"Don't hurry to notify them. Wait until we get in touch with his relatives. Depending on what they decide, we hand over the case or we solve it quietly."

The reasons of my suggestion are simple and harmless: the telephone where they called was a direct line, whereas the other calls went through the dispatch and then redirected to us, and if "papa" is loaded with money but doesn't appear in the newspapers at all, this means he's searching for maximum discretion.

"I got it. I'll try to localize the phone call."

"How haven't I thought of that, Cezar? Most definitely they called me from Grandma's house and they're now preparing a cake, so when we tear down the door with the ram, they greet us with cheers. They've used a mobile prepaid card and thrown it away afterwards"

"How do you know?"

"Before I joined law enforcement I was a professional kidnapper, but I had to quit because during the same period I was taking ballet lessons and the schedules overlapped."

Already, in my mind arise the first questions. A kidnapping in Craiova and they call the capital? And why have the kidnappers called us directly? They probably knew the police would be called and wanted to get a jump start, but why the number in my office? They seem clever enough. Why did they take this young boy? People with money can be found in all corners. And why does this Badea guy have nightclubs when he's bringing him barrels of money from oil? And, after all, who is this Mihai Badea?

A tearing pain strikes the back of my head. The "rag" on the desk rang exactly like the one at home. Oh, how I hate this sound! Cezar answers like a secretary who sleeps with her boss and she knows that she won't be fired, no matter what.

"The National Inspectorate of Forensics, Cezar speaking. Who do I have the pleasure of speaking to?"

I am such an idiot! That's why the name sounds familiar! And my thoughts begin to find tongue.

"Dip me in chocolate, kid, and feed me to the lesbians!"

"Boss?"

"This Badea guy called me the other day to help him find his mutt..."

"... yes, it's all right, he will contact you. Have a nice day. What, boss?"

"Nothing. Prepare some supplies for me. I'm leaving for Craiova. Actually, no ... you're coming with me. We leave on the first train!"

"Well, boss, I ... I mean, I must get packed ..."

"Nonsense, child! We will get aboard the iron horse with nothing else. It's just a courtesy visit!"

"But..."

"You convinced me, we're packing.

After I knock the kid into shape, I call Badea senior to break down the news, in case he hasn't heard already ...

"Mister Badea?"

"Yes, who is it?"

"Mister Badea Mihai?"

"Yes, it is me, who am I speaking to?"

"Settle down, get something hard to sit on if you are weak of heart. I have decided to help you. This is Dan, Demetriad Dan. You called me a few days ago about your mutt ... about your dog ..."

"So you accept, you'll search for my dog? Or what ... you got me confused ..."

"Well, until we get to the dog, we still need to find something else ... you haven't received any suspicious phone calls?"

"No, at least I don't think so. I was in a meeting and haven't got the chance to check my phone calls ... whatever ... it doesn't matter. Why are you asking?"

"Well, a nobody called us today and told us that your son was kidnapped from the train station ..."

"This can't be! He left this morning for Sibiu ..."

"He didn't get the chance to leave. At the moment I cannot give you any more details, but I am heading hastily to Craiova and we will be able to discuss it there."

"I cannot believe this ... when will you arrive? It doesn't matter. Give me a call when you are in Craiova. I will come pick you up."

"Perfect." I hang up and I stare at Cezar, who is writing down various things in a pocket notebook. I'm never curious to see what he's writing, but I'll wait until he'll pass the half of the notebook, so I will have a longer reading and, hopefully, full of smiles.

The rest of the day I spent in a coffee house, where I tried to make connections among the problems. My problems were that Ingrid was shy and I wasn't succeeding in convincing her to withdraw with me in my den, waiting for the train. Ingrid is a simple girl, with big green eyes, slightly curly hair, and the color of mad wind. She speaks little, but to my understanding. She is a person who appreciates common sense, affection, deep feelings. It seems as if I don't have enough time to convince her, so I settle on exchanging only a few words with her and making her understand that I will return from where I'm going, and she can't escape.

One hour later, Cezar informs me that he's already at the train station, waiting for me to leave. I throw a few extra clothes in a bag and I leave. There was the option to leave by a police car, but I prefer not to stand out in relief, and a train ride can do no harm. Arriving at the train station, I notice that it is too crowded and cramped, even though it would take more than ten minutes to cross it from one end to another even if I was the only passenger. Cezar looks exactly like a tourist prepared for an adventure in the jungle. He smiles when he sees me walking through the crowd, and his face very much resembles that of a happy dog. His face is banal; his beard isn't yet thick enough to call him a man, and his eyes are symmetrically positioned on both sides of his bottle nose. His haircut is like that of a schoolboy, and he has messy hair, and I've never seen him use any sort of hair gel or other products to enhance his look. He's very common, as I told you earlier. I grab my suitcase by the handle and we go toward the fire horse, which was patiently expecting for us, making a weird noise once in a while. To my luck, the railways have had the common sense to replace the old sheet metal wagons, nicely painted by non-talented people, with new ones with sensored doors and plush seats.

"Look at how this technology evolved," I think mostly to myself.

"What do you mean?"

"Fifteen years ago, when I last travelled by train, we had cardboard tickets and wax cloth seats. And the ride itself made you feel like in a *montagne russe*." And this started an incredibly boring conversation, which, if I start to detail, you'll hate me for even before you have the chance to know me, so I will get over it. Over Cezar. With my eyes. I see a thing. It's a man, and he's alone. I get up and head toward him.

"Is this seat taken?" I ask, pointing to one of the seven free seats out of eight possible around him.

"Yes."

"Thank you." I sit down on the one in front of him. My gesture doesn't surprise him at all. I throw my eyes out the window, watching the piles and trees racing past the train.

"Where are you heading?" I ask, trying to animate him.

"That way!" He points out toward the direction in which the train is going. Cezar, who has been quietly assisting our entire pseudo-discussion, has now moved to my seat for a better view of us two.

"One day, we all go, but, if you don't mind, can I ask for more details on your destination?"

"Are you an idiot?" He surprises me, looking at me for the first time.

I lift my eyebrow in suspicion and take my hand toward the pocket where I have my tribal chief ID. I dig my hand deep and take out a pack of gum.

"Here, maybe this will sweeten your words."

"You are still an idiot," he continues, turning his head to the window in an automatic gesture. The grave tone, perfectly straight mouth, and short, clean beard give him an air of seriousness. You could swear that this man was not capable of transmitting any kind of feelings through his features. His eyes are naturally beetle-browed, and he looks through under his eyebrows, just as natural. He looks just like Rasputin. "In this case, I feel I have to take attitude, my dear snail head!"

I stand up and I combine my body's position with a serious face and slightly risen chin, all together worthy of a Rembrandt painting.

"You haven't forgotten, after more than ten years."

He refers to the period spent in the academy, when I was waiting for him for tens of minutes anywhere we had to go, and not because he was doing something interesting that held him but because this reflected his interest in the world. And since he looked just like a man, I couldn't call him simply "snail," so I only used his head. The rigid background so far was dissipating somewhere behind. Cezar was breathing in relief. The guy in front of me is a good friend, as you by now will have understood, a former colleague in the academy. Only he opted for psychology. He was always fascinated by this field. Personally, I think it comes from his old man.

A massive and quiet man, a front-line war veteran. Only five men in his platoon survived, but he was left with sequelae, which he never succeeded in overcoming. It's understandable, considering the situation. I relate to this aspect in order to start a conversation with him, on a less aggressive note than earlier.

"The old man?"

"Gone."

"Long gone?"

"It's been around three years."

"Too bad, he was a good man."

"Yes. Unfortunately, I haven't managed to find out too much from him from that period. He used to smile and say, 'Nothing much happened there, son. It was like a day at the harvest."

"That's weird. You lived in the city."

"Exactly. Can you imagine what happened out there?"

"I'm trying. It's agonizing. Where did your life end up?"

"Nowhere. He was my purpose. I have failed. Now I work for the police, but the cases in which they need my help are rare."

"That's right, they don't make serial killers like they used to. Now you barely encounter a slightly crueler assassin, because the rest work by the book. And now where to?"

"Timisoara. I'm going to visit my sister."

"You didn't have a sister."

"I still don't. Does it matter?"

"Like a grandma in a striptease club."

We exchange a few more road impressions, and afterwards I return to my seat. I stare out the window, trying not to think of what's expecting me. And plus, what should I think of, since with all the clues I hold so far I could very well make a vanilla pudding. The train slowly continues its journey, and my only thought at the moment sits tight in an XXL coffee.

In Craiova, we exit in front of the train station, where I throw myself like a hyena of the coffee vending machine. With one claw I huddle the banknote in its spot, and with the other I search for the pack of cigars in my pocket. Unfortunately, I only find my mobile phone, which I hate as much as the one at home and the one from work, and so on. I am even horrified by the technology nowadays! I feel violated, and there is no moment in which one cannot find out where I am. Most times, I avoid answering, or I answer selectively, using my mood as criterion for selecting interlocutors. I peacefully take my coffee and enjoy its flavor. I feel things will go all right. Returning to the initial problems, I press "call." I hear Badea on the other end of the line, confirming his presence in the train station in approximately two minutes. I think he has his teleportation badge on him. I burn a cigarette and I start smoking like a steam engine going bored round the yard line.

A 4x4 pulls near me and lowers its window. Inside, another 4x4, only human this time.

"Mister Demetriad."

He "What a coincidence, I'm also Demetriad!"

"Get in, please, and let's go."

"How come?"

"Excuse me?"

"How would it be if I was getting in any car which pulls near me, like hoity-toity! At least if you were of the opposite sex and if your intentions weren't entirely orthodox."

"Excuse me. I am Mihai Badea."

"I knew it all along, but I wasn't sure I can smoke in your car, so I stalled for finishing my cigar. Damn … where are my manners? This is Cezar. He will accompany me during this investigation."

"Delighted!"

"Let's not overreact, time is extremely valuable! Let's go!" I reply before Cezar can even respond to his "delight."

We board the "ship" and head for one of the clubs, I assume. After parking the Goliath in front of an imposing two-story building made of smoky glass and possessing a slightly strange geometry, with two primates carefully wrapped in suits guarding the doors, my first thought was, *Money laundering! This really is going to be exciting.*

We pass by the primates, who, amazingly, knew how to articulate words and had greeted us with a "hm-mm" and an indistinguishable head movement, as though they were paid to do nothing. On the ground level, on the left side there were some tastefully ordered snugs, and on the right the snugs from the left were continued, giving the room some symmetry.

Spotlights and colorful light bulbs, so specific to clubs, were missing. Instead, a few speakers big enough to accommodate a family of two were spread through the room. By their appearance, I'm sure they were used for resuscitating patients. Two to three "bum" and already the patient would have started breathing. Straight ahead was the bar. We are heading toward it when, only two meters from the espresso machine on the counter, Mihai turns right on the stairs. If I wasn't so curious as to where we are going, I would stay here, with the espresso machine as my hostage and all doors locked.

We go upstairs and enter a room that extends the entire level of the floor. Here the furniture is visibly more expensive, and the design very much resembles a living room—a couch in the center of the room, a glass table in front of it, and a few meters away a television set proportional in size to the owner's body mass. We left the pool table behind and approached the corner, where a sculpted wooden bar was supporting fine drinks and things needed for an interminable party. You could tell that that was the place where the man discussed business and gurgled tons of alcohol with buddies. It was a sort of private club mixed with a futuristic residence, and I am sure that not more than twenty persons have seen its interior. Now I have the time to study it more careful. Although I'm almost two meters height, next to this guy I look like a Brussels sprout sitting next to a robust garden cabbage. In order for you to visualize its dimensions, think of the Arc de Triomphe , only not empty inside. His big, broad shoulders suggest that the man has been a long-time sportsman, his chest more lavish and more firm than that of most women, and a glare that causes back pain when fixed upon you. A young lady enters through the same door as us—at least that's how she appears—small in stature, with a fair blond hair, blue eyes in which I've seen the Pacific and part of the Atlantic, and a voice that can stop even a kangaroo in heat from jumping.

"Hello, I'm Cristina, Mihai's wife. And you are …?"

"Dan, but you can call me Demetriad. I don't want any confusion. I really don't feel the need to disturb Mr. Badea. Although that would mean that I'd die happy. Delighted. This is Cezar."

I'm tired of always introducing the kid. People will think he's dumb and deaf, but it's all for the best. He's programmed such that every two useful words, he'll bring the rest of the discussion to ruin.

"Good, let's not waste any more time. First of all, I want to know if this investigation will be official right from the beginning or I will notify the police when we have something concrete."

"I'd rather we start in a discrete manner. It's possible that the situation will be solved rather quickly. Or it may be just a joke."

"Understood. No problem. I's always best not to make a racket about a kidnapping, lest you alert those responsible for the disappearance. Most of them panic and will do anything to getting rid of the evidence. Since it's a kidnapping we're talking about, the biggest evidence would be your son."

"Yes, I'm aware of that, that's why I would like a private investigation, of course, to the extent possible."

"Again, understood. Now let's take a load off our minds. Let's determine exactly what you expect from me."

"Maximum discretion, for which I can offer fifty thousand euros when the case is closed."

"Clear enough. Now let's discuss what has happened. I understood that Marius' cell phone is turned off, which confirms our anonymous tip. Have you tried contacting his colleagues, or the coach?"

"We don't have their numbers, and we didn't have the time to go to the gym."

"And you won't. I will handle things from now on. Now you'll have to give me a few details abo—"

"Good evening."

She interrupted me! I hate being interrupted. By the sound of it, I figured she's of the fair sex, my own species, but facing her I realize that I was wrong. She's not of the fair sex. She's of the as much sex as possible! But still she interrupted me, and I try to continue.

"Good evening. Dan Demetriad is my name," and I reach out my hand to touch hers, which was latently vaguely propped on her hip.

"Good evening, I'm Alina."

Hmm, my hand, suspended in the air, is now making its course to the head and begins to rub the smattering of hair that has grown since my last haircut. I look at her, raising one of my eyebrows. Her gesture indicates inconceivable arrogance. She's got some nerve. She looks at me and superciliously begins a conversation.

"So you're Dan, and what are you doing here?"

"Well, fair lady, I—"

"I'm no madam, no lady, and it would be polite of you to address me as miss. So … what's your business?

"I'm from the gas company."

"This building is not branched to the gas network."

"Damn, I've been uncovered! You got me. I'm from the electricity company."

"Alina, stop it. Mister Demetriad is here because Marius is missing." Mihai intervened.

"Missing where? He's in Sibiu," she replies while heading for the bar.

I stand still and keep my eye on her. Tall, with long legs, she has the walk of a tigress ready to strike, her hair in a ponytail flowing down her neck. Her tight shirt, as if it was hastily bought from the children's department, emphasizes her shapes. Gently, she dibs me with her shoulder passing and casts through her lips a "sorry" that I wouldn't forgive at any price. I was ready for an acid answer to melt her confidence , I take a deep breath and ...

"Hi, Bogdan!" someone says when I was about to take charge.

Ah ... and I was so close! I forgot about her companion, a small, chubby guy with no visible flaws, long hair, a thick beard covering his throat, and a warm, soft voice. I look at him, surprised.

"Hi! But, you ... do this often?"

"What?" He replies, rattled.

"Nothing important. I was having a revelation, a premonition." I reply sparing myself of a long and useless explanation. Besides, how can I explain something I haven't said.

"Does this mean that you are also a medium?" Alina replies from behind the bar, where she was preparing her drink, a sign that she is used to the atmosphere here.

"Of course, I managed to predict the Great Plague in England and the Second World War, before I even read about them."

Frankly, in such cases I'd be capable of convinving someone to believe in seashells that morphs into rhinos, just so I'm right." I assume a grave glare, solemnly sit down on the couch, and, with a cigar between my teeth, try to start the discussion, as comforting as possible.

"It's very nice to meet you, and honestly, I would have enjoyed meeting Marius too, but unfortunately he was retained, literally, with some problems. When was the last time you spoke to him, Mr. Badea?"

"Today, before he left for Sibiu, but after that I didn't manage to get a hold of him. I thought that probably he left his phone in the room, or who knows what he did."

"He's a rebellious teenager, riggish, not really caring for anything, giddy." Says Alina

"All due respect, Miss Alina, I believe his parents are more entitled to give us his psychological profile."

"No, it's all right. She's right about him; we haven't really taken care of his education. Most of his friends can be found, hanging around bars and clubs at all hours, spending their parents' money. Nothing in particular, just sleep and fun."

"I understand … it's some sort of turbo-vegetable, only with his propellers clogged, not really helping him climb the evolutionary ladder."

"Would you like something to drink?" the voice behind the bar echoes.

"No, thank you. I give up alcohol a long time ago, mostly forced by circumstances."

Of course they'll never find out about the episode when, groggy and in the mood for life, I broke into my own home because I couldn't take the key off the key chain. During watering the bushes grown on the bottom of my water closet, I was writing two hand-written reports to myself—one for destruction of property and the other for the brutal way in which I handled the beast. I managed to analyze and cancel them both the following morning, while the pumpkin, heavily held on my shoulders, was dangling just like the pendulum of a clock. I should've written three, considering the abominable language I used on myself.

"However, I would like a coffee, if it's not too much to ask."

While quietly sipping the hot espresso, those around me were very focused on discussing absolutely nothing. I saw the opportunity to bring some logic to the situation. I still had nothing concrete about the kid, and I was thinking that I should get more details about his father. Something is telling me that is was revenge, the result of not-exactly-legitimate business practices. But this raises another question: Will Badea be willing to share his not so legal businesses with me and tell me everything? Maybe this will give me a starting point for my search, but he will also have to bear the consequences. An idea brutally struck me! Alina, she must know what's going on, since she's close to the family. I finish my coffee and I inform the hosts about my intention to go to the hotel for a few hours of quietness.

"We can accommodate you. Here you have a guest room where you can stay for as long as needed.

"Thank you for the offer, but I prefer the comfort of a hotel. You know how it is, room service, smiling young ladies cleaning my dirt, and plus, all expenses are borne by the inspectorate." I get up, and Cezar follows my example. I slowly approach the bar, where Alina still potters.

"Please give me a pack of cigars."

"I don't think you've noticed, but here we don't sell. It's a private bar."

"I don't think you've noticed, but I didn't say that I want to buy."

Her eyes turn big for a moment; she probably didn't expect the boldness I am displaying. I reach out to grab it and subtly offer in exchange a business card, which she throws in her jacket pocket without any reaction.

"Call me. I want to meet and discuss a few things."

"I take it you're inviting me out?"

"Yes, but it's for business; the meeting is official."

"Believe me, otherwise I would not have honored your invitation."

With these last few words she smiles, vixenish, slightly distinguishable. I slowly turn to the others, just to say good-bye, and after we head for the stairs. Back on the street, we decide to leave for the hotel.

I think it's been more than ten years since I last visited Craiova. I came with my old man, searching for a contact person who would put us in touch with a big weapon collector. We were both under cover, my dad, an FID[2] officer, was impersonating a devoted hunter, and I was the son in search of his identity.

Maybe we would have even succeeded if our contact person hadn't succeeded in dying in a crossfire.

We decided to spend a few more days in the area, to admire the landscape. Very few things were different, maybe a few new stores, and people older by ten years. Cezar has been trying to understand my stare. He quickly gives up and starts to ferment next to me.

"Where are we heading, boss?"

"Well, firstly at the hotel, to take over out beds, and the first thing tomorrow morning we'll go looking for a rental hauler. It's more useful than two feet. Let's go, my border guards! "

"We're alone."

"That's just a detail. Follow me. I know a hotel with a nice view to the sky, if you're looking up, and to the ground, if you're looking down."

---

2 FID—Foreign Information Department

We checked in a hotel with four stars painted at its entrance, in separate rooms of course. I'm not going to spend my time alone out here, and the idea of a ménage-a-trois with my recruit does not excite me at all.

In the morning, after filling our gut with nutrients, namely two strong coffees, we went looking for a hauler. We signed for a large SUV. It's very handy when you're distraught by the view; you don't get concerned when a pole jumps in front of you. While running in the mastodon, the phone, deeply hidden in the pocket, began roaring. I answer, without even caring that it might be a formal discussion.

"So, yes! So, me! So who are you?"

"Dan?"

"According to recent research, himself."

"It's Alina … I found your business card in my pocket, and since I have some free time, I thought of calling you."

"And it's a good thing you did. I also don't have anything interesting on my agenda. Do you think we could meet?" Yes, I know, I was very direct and skipped a few stages, but it's preferable to be brief and concise when you want to avoid awkward moments.

"Yes, let's say around ten? In the Arcade Club?"

"Of course, it's perfect. I don't know where that is, but there's no building on Earth which cannot be found, so we'll speak then if it's all right. At the moment I'm caught up in some problems."

I hang up and I lay more comfortably in my seat. The traffic light shows I have twenty more seconds to wait. I look at my watch and it indicates it's almost two. I had to fill the time with something as I waited for the evening to come, so I decided, unanimously with myself, to head toward nowhere, killing time. The day passed rather quickly, considering that all we did was driving around with no particular target. The same watch now indicates it's eight.

"Kid, I'm going to take you back to the hotel so you can go through the Constitution and Human Rights, all right?"

"But why, boss?"

"Well, because, first of all, you're not very good when it comes to applicable legislation, and secondly because you have an article there regarding the 'right to privacy,' which I am fully going to take advantage of!"

"So why can't I also come with you?"

"All right, you convinced me. I'm also going to buy an explicative dictionary so you can completely understand the meaning of the word 'privacy'!"

"If you say so ..."

We're heading for the hotel, where I throw my clothes on the floor and myself in the shower, trying to get a new look. I put on something more somber and go down in front of the hotel. I call a taxi driver and place my order. He looks at me baffled, while I step away from his car and catapult myself into my mastodon. I follow him closely, and once we got in front of the club, I go and honor my order, as the model citizen that I am.

It looks like I'm here too early. I go in and look towards a table in the corner, sufficiently illuminated so I can look at my companion, but sufficiently twilit so I can hide my stare. I order a double black coffee, sufficiently strong that the finest pastry cooks would label it as a pudding. While I was flirting with the young lady that came to satisfy my needs, strictly those on the menu, I see her walking in the darkness of the club. Black leather boots and pants. I move my eyes up and, after a long road, I see her thighs. Her pants are tight and fit her body so well that one can see the line of her underwear. I force my eyeballs and subtly look at her abdomen, exposed by a blouse that could easily be considered a bra. Her hands are tucked in the jacket's pockets, also made of leather, of course, perfecting a wonderful view. At the risk of rolling my eyes over my head, I glare, searching for her breasts. I am unsuccessful, however; I would have to be a snail for that. Now I raise my head and stare her in the eyes. Interesting.

She takes a seat opposite of me and assumes a comfortable position. I throw my elbows on the table, just enough to smell her perfume. Hm-mm ... Cacharel, Eden. Unmistakable scent. She looks at the lady with the menu and dispatches her rapidly.

"Hello, please bring me a coffee."

"Right away, Alina."

"Welcome!" I say and she smiles ironically.

"Let's get over formalities. Tell me, is this discussion being taped, or are you taking notes?"

"You watch too many movies. Official discussion doesn't mean that I'm going to put a light in your face and you'll tell me everything you know. It only means that I won't start paying you dozens of compliments, in hope that one of them will convince you to come with me at the hotel for a night among fluffy clouds."

"I don't like clouds."

"So far."

"What makes you think that I'd change my opinion?"

"Experience. We're all made of the same material."

"Just the packaging is the same; the content is different."

"So? Anyway, we all function according to the same laws. And there are bitter punishments for damaging the packaging."

"Only if you're not capable of avoiding them, or using them to your own advantage."

"I didn't mean the written ones. I'm talking strictly about the laws of the Universe. In all there is a balance, which will sooner or later be reached. Returning to the subject, I saw that you have a good relationship with the Badea family. Have you known each other for a long time?"

"Yes, very long, I believe I was about fourteen years old when my parents sold the apartment in Craiova and moved to a rural area. I wanted to stay in town, finish high school, and go to faculty. My father was a good friend of Mihai and talked to him, so I could stay in one of his apartments."

"Nice gesture, but still, Mihai doesn't seem the selfless type."

The girl bringing coffee interrupted my sequence of words while pushing the coffee on the table.

"Can I get you anything else?"

"Not for now, and if it's possible that nobody disturbs us, perfect" Alina says to her, and the girl nods and turns around.

"Do all medical students own clubs, or are you one of the few most fortunate?"

Her eyes got the shape of watermelons treated with plenty of fertilizer. She was probably intrigued about how I found out so quickly who she is and what she does. Nothing complicated here. When I spoke to her on the phone, in the background I managed to distinguish voices of persons talking in medical terms about the fact that their hands still had that specific color, left by talcum powder and sweat inside surgical gloves, which led me to believe that she's still a student. In the club, the waiting girl was shaking when she saw her, and the coffee was brought in cups different from the others I saw on another table, which indicated that she's an important person around here. She takes a deep breath and answers.

"During high school, Mihai saw that I'm a resourceful girl, enterprising, and proposed a business. He establishes a club for me, in my name, and I undertake that in five years I restitute the entire amount invested, and ten percent of incomes afterwards."

"Nice gesture," I repeat with an idiotic automatism, because I was busy trying to find the motive, besides the obvious one, money laundering, of the human SUV. It seems he holds an enormous amount of money, besides the official one.

"And Marius? It's him we're talking about, let's not forget that the poor child is held somewhere, fed from dirty dishes by starving criminals, who would probably feed on each other, if their religion wouldn't prohibit it. "

"He was like a younger brother. When I met him first, he was three years old, and since I was spending most of my time around the Badea family, he was like a brother."

"And what was he doing now in Sibiu?"

"He went at a training camp, practicing for a boxing contest in September."

"Was he practicing boxing for a long time?"

"I believe it's been four years since he started boxing, because when I returned from France, he already had a few trophies."

Our discussion slowly became friendly, which is exactly what I intended. I deduced that she was about twenty-seven years old, and she told me that she's still a student, because she spent two years in France and had to interrupt studies. I found out that her parents died four years before, in a car accident, and the inheritance her father left her was a big hole in the pocket, debt that she managed to cover so far. She is single, and Bogdan is the man helping her manage the club. The rest is irrelevant. Toward the end I concluded, "Unfortunately, I have to leave. Tomorrow I have a busy day. Can I take you somewhere?"

"If it's not too much to ask, you could leave me somewhere uptown? I still have something to solve before going home."

We step out of the club and get in the rental SUV. We pass by my hotel and continue, going uptown. She asks me to stop in front of a one-story house, illuminated by an entire arsenal of garden lamps with solar batteries. She drily greets me and leaves. It's 1-0 for me! When I got out of club I noticed that the same car was parked as the one parked in front of Badea's clubhouse a day before, and since she was the only thing in common, it definitely belonged to her, so when she accepted my offer, she actually intended to say, "Yes, I'll come with you, but if you want me to come up, you have to insist a little more." Besides that, seeing that we passed my hotel, she realized that nothing was going to happen, so she asked me to drop her off anywhere, leaving the impression that that's the place where she has something to solve. Actually, she just wanted to catch a taxi and return to get her car. All this started when I looked her in the eye. Her eyes gave her away.

After returning to the hotel, I find Cezar sleeping and drooling in my room, which makes me think. This guy is either my mother and wants to check when I come back home, he's in love with me, or he's an idiot. I open the minibar and dip into a bottle of wine. I'm alone. I can afford to drink without making a fool of myself, and plus, I have to moist and my thoughts so I can combine them easier.

I pour a large glass of wine and fill a bowl found in the bathroom with cold water, then return to the room. It's time for tests! I get his lethargic hand from under his head and put it on the edge of the bowl, with fingers in the water … and I wait … and I wait … and nothing happens. It's probably a myth that one pees on himself if you perform the above mentioned act on him.

Nothing I know so far connects. Mihai is irritatingly indifferent regarding his own child. Cristina hasn't even asked about him, even if he's not her child, confirmed by the fact that she's been living with Mihai for three years at most. She doesn't wear a wedding ring and she has the attitude of a normal, modest person, not bossy. I bet they're not even legally married. This would help Badea use her bank accounts to deposit some amounts which he can't justify if they were in his own accounts. It's her I should speak to more. She's honest and open. I finish my second glass of wine and head for the telephone in the room.

"How do you do, miss. Can you bring some food to my room?"

"Of course. What exactly would you be interested in?"

"Well, I'd like a jar of strawberry jam. Actually, no, I want some marmalade. In fact, some yogurt would do it."

And that guy, Bogdan, is clearly one of the guys performing the dirty work. He doesn't seem so smart, but still, he must be up to some good …

Ding! I have an idea! No, the ding was on the door. My yogurt is here. What a look on the young lady carrying the tray. I sniffed her fear of rape from miles away, and taking advantage of the physical trauma of delivering yogurt at 2 a.m., I smile to her.

"Don't you want to come in and enjoy a bit of yogurt?"

She smiles, forced by the internal regulations, and politely declines, according to the same regulations, motivating that she's working.

I remove the cap on the yogurt and I taste it. It's of the finest quality. I'm sure Cezar will enjoy it! I open the slit of his pants and pour the entire cup inside, which doesn't seem to bother him one bit, so I take the bowl of water and pour it on his face, while yelling,

"On your stomach, soldier. It's shoal water!"

"Boss, you're ba ... pfpfbleahpff ..."

I deem that he's not really able to speak while water floods his mouth.

"Cezar, you must get used to working in difficult conditions! Now, get up and off to your room. I can't think with you here!"

He gets up, a bit ashamed by the situation, and wishes me goodnight while heading for the door. Drips of water are running off him, and small drops of yogurt are running down from his left leg."

I sip a couple glasses of wine more, make the bed, and then quietly go to sleep in the armchair. You never know who's going to wind up in your room...

Chapter II
Or the chapter immediately after the first

I reserve my second day for a walk with Badea. I wanted to look like a personal reporter, following his celebrity anywhere in hopes of a revelation, or a beautiful landscape against which to pose so that the moment is not lost. Yes, it happens only once in six months but that doesn't matter. He has an enviable salary, and that's enough. The difference is that I was gathering clues, if any. I leave the hotel after having a strong coffee; otherwise, I think I would have crawled like a turtle to the reception, where I would have been intubated and taken over by medics. I can almost see them around me. "Charge! Clear! Crggg. We have a pulse, stat, 500CC serum with 25 percent caffeine. His awakening is in our hands!"

I choose to walk so I can render to Cezar the SUV. This way he won't get bored and disturb me. Who knows, maybe he wishes to take an outlaw walk in search of hermits in the woods in the area, and could really use the Hulk. I get to Badea's house rather quickly, and he seems to have just awakened and from the look in his eyes I can tell his mind flooded with thoughts. Something tells me it's not about the boy. Considering the amount of time they were spending together, I don't think he even noticed that he's missing. Noon is here already, and we didn't even left the house. I thought I made a really stupid choice. Instead of searching for things that would have helped me, I was assisting to family chats going from why the toilet paper no longer has lemons drawn on it to if the mailman should ring or not the doorbell more, before leaving the invoices in the mail box …

"I think it would be better if the mailman would bring them himself."

"Anyway, Cristina, it's not you the one who pays them, so I don't understand why you bother so much."

"I know, but again we'll be facing the situation where our phones don't work because someone forgot to pay them."

I was very interested in the discussion. They have even proposed to pay the guy from the Postal Office separately, just to make sure all invoices get to where they're needed. These are essential things for the investigation. Maybe we can't contact Marius because his telephone invoice hasn't been paid. God, I am so bored! The only thing that keeps me from losing my head is my strategic position a hand away from the espresso machine, not letting my cup get empty for even one second. I see Mihai getting dressed. There's a good chance we might go somewhere. I was right—in ten minutes we are already at the door of his *Enterprise*, waiting for the teleporter to board us on the ship. That didn't happen. Bip-bip and we open the door. Then we head for a more withdrawn lounge, where we can talk like men. As usual, I choose the most comfortable position, with visibility over the entire lounge. The Big B sits in front of me and opens the discussion.

"Honestly, I was expecting this."

"What, the lounge to be empty?" I answer in an idiotic fashion.

"No, Marius to disappear."

"So why didn't he have bodyguards with him?"

"Because it's one thing to expect it and another for it to actually happen. It was a risk I thought I could assume."

"And why was this expected?"

"Off the record?"

"For now I'm getting paid as a private detective. There is, however, a confidentiality guaranteed by the contract, which I cannot officially use. So you can tell me whatever you think is relevant."

"Over the last three years, my businesses has flourished, and many competitors have ended up in a gum tree."

"And the gum tree up in the air …"

"Exactly. And they've tried, by different means, to settle some old scores. From cars thrown in the river to threatening letters. I gave them a dose of their own medicine. And many of them were silenced."

"And what kind of medicine is that, exactly?"

"Violence under different forms, from simple beating to houses in flames."

"That works around the Olympic Games, and you can blame the Olympic flame. But still, family has come in the middle. Do you suspect anybody?"

"No, unfortunately there are too many, and it very well may be none of them."

"Good, then at least the worst of them."

"I can think of no one for the moment. And honestly, I didn't thought too much about it."

A passerby props his bicycle on the mist in my stomach. That's a sign that we should change locations and eat something. We get up without interrupting our talk and head for the car.

"Which is the maximum amount you could pay in exchange for the boy? I mean, if they called tomorrow, would you have the money for ransom?"

"Yes, in cash I have a little over half a million euros."

"I don't think they'll ask for that much. I don't know if a man who resorts to kidnapping can count more than two hundred thousands. The problem would be if they had access to a counting machine. However, I suppose this money has a rather dubious origin, like the circuit of water in nature—if it doesn't rain in abundance, it stays at a low level."

"It's correct, but this happened a long time ago. I now have enough money so it makes itself. I started with little things, a bar and a lounge."

"Where you had an invoice for one bottle of whisky, which you sold for an entire month ..."

"Exactly, ten to twenty bottles per month, all of them sold in the name of the legally declared ones. Profit was huge. After that, I started in real estate, but a few months before prices started dropping I sold everything, and through a few connections I managed to buy some stocks in petrol."

"This seems to be a good restaurant. I heard they serve delicious chops, from pigs with pedigree, champions at grunting and one-hundred-meter hurdles."

"Fine, we'll stop here. But be informed that it's my treat."

"Then you can call me Dan."

He started laughing and stopped at the restaurant's entrance. The order would have fed an entire village in Africa, but since the food would have spoiled before I got it to them., I decided to gorge, like a hyena that had just grabbed an antelope.

"And Marius' mother?"

"Gone."

"Still on Earth?"

"No."

"Accident?"

"Heart attack."

"I'm sorry. Long time?"

"Since Marius was one year old."

"So you raised him on your own?"

"Mostly my mother, and after, Alina took care of him."

"She could handle school and Marius?"

"I was paying her, so it was like a job for her. She made time, so I had no issues with him. Anyway, she was smart even then and managed to do anything."

"She must have discovered the secret of the thirty-six-hour day. Rudy?"

"Rudy was Marius' idea. He got bored by himself and wanted a dog. The choice of breed was also his."

"What breed?"

"Rottweiler."

"How long have you had it?"

"Almost two years, but I didn't really get along with it. Marius was the only one it listened to, and the dog was going haywire when it couldn't find Marius around the house. Fortunately, it wasn't too aggressive and never attacked anyone."

"Feature which seems that had cost it."

"Hmm, seems so."

The telephone began shaking the table. Luckily, it was his. He picks it up, looks at it for a second, and then answers rather shyly.

"Hi, tell me."

"…"

"Yes, it's all right. I'll be there in about half an hour. I'll be with a collaborator of mine. Thank you."

"Short, concise, and to the point, as far as I can see" I tell him as he puts his phone back on the table, so he doesn't have much time to fabricate any lies.

"As discussed, I rely on your utmost discretion."

First he refused to get involved with the police regarding the disappearance of his own son, then the amount offered for the case and the assertiveness of utmost discretion show that he still has certain businesses that police shouldn't know about because that would cost him a few years in a room with three walls, and the forth one made of steel bars. I have a feeling that I'll get some spicy details from where we're going. I love complicated situations.

"As long as our activity will help me solve this case, I'll use my short-term memory and everything that's happening here will remain between us."

"Perfect, then let's go. We're expected."

I have no idea where we're going or what will happen there. He pays the bill and we're going back to the car. On the way, as expected, I start asking questions.

"Who am I, actually?"

"A collaborator."

"I wouldn't have guessed. But what exactly is this about? I make bronze statues? Mechanically debone chicken? Mow the lawn in front of city hall?"

"No explanations will be needed. I never attend such meetings accompanied by persons whom I don't absolutely trust. This will definitely excuse you from any suspicious questions from them."

"Them? And who are they?"

"Some collaborators."

"I'm completely enlightened. Anyway, it's a good thing that people collaborate around here."

I carefully look out the window at the electrical poles that quickly pass. We leave the city and head to a motel, where we align our car with the others. I think this is a meeting of the Knights of the Round Table, the modern version, after discovering the four-cycle engine. The interior yard is covered by artificial lawn, and somewhere in the corner a wooden belfry keeps guard to a brick erection, nicely adorned with griller utensils. There are no customers on the left side of the restaurant. I like the interior décor. The wallpaper makes it look classic, and the wooden tables and chairs give it an even more attractive aspect. We pass by it and head to a completely different room. All is white, as if designed so that nothing would distract you from thinking. It's a room that doesn't seem to belong here, seeming cut out from a medical magazine. Besides the white around us, two windows, also white, allow the smoke to get out, and the round table in the middle is filled with glasses, chips, and playing cards. The four players are patiently waiting for us to join the game. We are briefly greeted with their wine glasses and then invited to take our seats. I see the people take the game very seriously, since one of them gives me his seat so I wouldn't stand next to Badea, a safety measure that I consider exaggerated. I receive a fist of colorful chips, and fortunately, I know the value of each one, so I cannot make a fool of myself on the first hand. One of the players stands up and starts throwing us cards. After several glasses of wine, everyone is relaxed; however, they become more intense—stakes are rising and bluffs are being made for thousands of Euros. I'm quietly playing my cards so I wouldn't stand out. I'm just one of the players, while Badea and two others are scenting and studying their every move, observing for any change of expression, any gesture that might give away the cards they have. I'm doing the same, observing and studying, analyzing any affirmation, or piece of conversation. Nothing interesting, and I was already under the impression that I'm losing my time here. I feel as though I can't see the forest because of the trees. My luck changes when one of the players places all his chips and loses. He gets up from the table, politely excuses himself, and leaves. We peacefully resume our game, and after a few hands without luck, Badea also stands up and addresses the group.

"Unfortunately, you'll have to play your next hand without me. I have to use the bathroom."

I feel like I ran out of luck, and not on the table. All who remained at the table are looking at me out of the tail of their eye, trying to find something out. I'm glad that no one dares to ask. Returning to the table, Badea sits back and loses his entire amount during the next hand.

"We'll have to leave. It's getting rather late, and we still have some things to solve before we head home. Thank you, gentlemen, for the poker night!"

Following his example, I get up and cash my chips.

We get in the car and head toward the city. Badea minds the road carefully, seeming like a model driver, who would have fooled me if I haven't had travelled by car with him until now. He was just upset, and something was telling me that Marius was not the reason.

"What did the guy want?"

"What guy?"

"The one who bet all his money on a hand which would have been lost in front of a pair of boots, totally opposite to his style of play so far, and who waited for you in the parking, just to leave with approximately twenty seconds before you retuned from the toilet. Honestly, I think that this was all that you wanted to find out, since when you returned you did your best to lose your money and leave."

"Is there anything you don't notice?" he replies, smiling and stunned.

"We all see it, but only a few of us really notice."

"Make me understand."

"It's simple. Were there wooden tables in the restaurant where we served lunch today?"

"Of course, they were all wooden."

"So you saw them! But how many were there?"

"How many? Why would I have counted them?"

"So that you'd notice them. There were twenty tables, out of which five had six seats each. This means a total of ninety seats in the restaurant. During our stay, only two other tables were occupied which would not have earned enough money to keep the restaurant open, but the fact that they have ninety seats shows that various organized events take place here, which produce enough so that the personnel are paid and the business keeps running."

"I already knew that."

"You knew because you have seen it, but have you ever noticed? So, what did the violent butcher who's being watched by the police want after all?"

"We had an older business, which I dropped out of, and now he wants us to resume it."

"I need your help in the investigation to the extent possible, and the fact that you're hiding certain details from me doesn't help, regardless if, from your point of view, they are or not connected to the investigation. I'm not interested in him, and I really am not going to investigate him. The police are handling this, anyway."

"But how do you know these things about him?"

"His left hand is crossed by marks from the chain glove *butchers* use for protection. And his index and middle finger had minor lesions from the fact that during meat carving, he hurts himself—either on the table or from bones—which leads me to believe he's no knight ready for crusades. It's normal that he's being monitored by the police, since he drives a luxury car and he's a simple butcher. And his violent nature is easy to observe. On his last arrest he made a little fuss, struggling quite a bit. Because they didn't want to use force , which they would have had to justify afterwards, the policemen handcuffed him tightly so each move would cause pain, which would be at least irritating. The signs on his wrists told me that.

"Now I understand why you are so famous. But I think sometimes there are things that you do't notice."

"Of course, but this only happens for a moment, and in the end things connect. Exactly like in this case. Our only problem is time. Also the fact that you still doubt my confidentiality only makes me wonder. I know this isn't about any deal you want to resume—it doesn't make sense."

"That's right. It's about a friend who was arrested recently and indicted. The situation is far from good for him; it's about a double crime, confinement and other charges. The problem is another—the connection in many situations. He had connections everywhere, and he was renowned for the firmness he proved when things needed to get solved."

I end the discussion and dive in a puddle of thoughts. "Maybe the life of a so-called mobster isn't as interesting as they say, or maybe I witnessed one of the monotonous days. Anyway, one thing is certain, Badea will not help the investigation in any way, because he's afraid of the repercussions, so I'll have to take care of this by myself."

With small and frequent tick-tocks, time was doing its best to send the sun to sunset. Badea observes that I'm agitated and says, "Let's see how things stand in the clubs. They are to be open soon, and I want to make sure everything is finished."

"A gym would have also been a good choice. Considering the quantity of cholesterol I have in me, there's the risk that my heart will go on a strike."

I was preparing to note today's discussion in the part of my brain responsible for storing information. During this entire time, our location changed drastically—from a chic restaurant to total darkness, slit by colorful beams. It was the two of us, and a horde of people. Security, barmen, dancers, and a few unidentified persons. Only now I've met Badea, the money maker. I saw that he's obsessed about cleanness and strict about money. The same story everywhere: screaming, shouting, and shards have put the staff in motion in all the clubs we went in. Six of them. The first two were "pathetic, trash, rack and ruin," quoting him, but the others were better and better. Probably telephones rang like in the White House in the other clubs and, knowing his demands, they fixed everything so Badea won't get annoyed. If that's the way he treated Marius, I'm surprised the kid turned seventeen around him. We conclude our tour and exchange a few meaningless words. Slightly past midnight I get to my hotel room, which this time is empty, especially of Cezar. I feel a bit betrayed, I would have liked him to be present when I take to my own thoughts and completely ignore him, but I settle on sitting in the armchair and, before I realize it, I fall into a deep sleep, lacking any kind of cerebral activity, conscious, unconscious, vestibular. Just sleep.

Chapter III
Or the one before the fourth

The coffee is here. I watch with my eyes half closed as the young lady enters the room, briefly scans the area and flinches when she realizes I'm on the armchair. She walked on her toes just to slam the coffee saucer on the table at the end. I mumble a strange noise, just like when you go into a cave to hide from the rain and from the inside some noises make you realize that it's better if you get wet.

The meeting, set for 8 a.m. was calculated from the start with one hour's delay, so I can peacefully enjoy my coffee. I forgot to mention it earlier, but I thought that since I'm in the area, I might as well take advantage and seem like a model Quaestor who is also interested in the official business and visit the Inspectorate. This is in appearance only, because in fact I only needed some information. Cezar knocks on my door at about 8:30, enters, and sits on the side of the bed, rubbing his eyes and yawning.

I clear the smoke and greet him. He mumbles an answer, then says, "Boss, did you manage to get anything from Miss Alina?"

"Well, Cezar, do you thing I went there for nothing? Of course I did! Her bra size is BB and she likes French perfumes."

"And what did Mr. Badea say?"

"That the clubs are a mess. What did you do yesterday?"

"I looked for you in your room, and you weren't there, and after that I tried calling you. Since I couldn't get through to you, I walked around the town and … that's about it. So, after all, what's going on?"

"I have the feeling that Marius was kidnapped, but I still don't know by whom," I reply with an idiotic grin.

"Cezar, today you have a special mission. After dropping me off at the Inspectorate, you'll take the car and look for Bogdan, the guy who was with Alina yesterday. This should help you," I say while taking out of the pocket a little paper on which I write legibly the phone number of the Information Service. "Look for an expensive veterinary office. You'll either find the doctor of the dog owned by the Badea family, or you'll find Bogdan. By the dog food I smelled when he came near me, it's definitely his occupation."

He takes the small piece of paper without any comments and we head for the car. At 9:30 sharp I arrive in front of the Inspectorate. Perfect! An hour and a half late, exactly as I planned. They're probably sitting comfortably, with their feet on the desks, cursing the false alarm that a Chief Quaestor is coming to visit. Exactly as I anticipated. My wedding guest suit works wonders. No one notices me in the building. Even more, two of the policemen inside are staring and I feel them wanting to grab me by the collar and implant me with some slaps, kick my rear, and then throw me out. I head straight to the local Chief's office, and as I go by the secretary, I order a strong coffee. I enter the office knocking on the door, but only after I've opened it wide. Against my expectations, I'm greeted with common sense.

"Hello, how may I help you?"

"My regards, Inspector. I want to report an act of sexual aggression."

"No problem. A colleague of mine will help you right away. Andr—"

"No!" I interrupt him. "I'd prefer if you'd help me yourself. You know … it's something intimate, and I'm sure that they'd make fun of me at the station."

"All right then, have a seat. What happened?"

"This morning, when I woke up, I got dressed for leaving, and at the hotel reception I met a very nice young lady. I couldn't help myself, and so I hovered for a chat. Things degenerated a bit, so I have the feeling that I aggressed her. This leads me to my other problem: I had an important meeting at eight, and I'm late."

"You take yourself too seriously. There's no need to worry regarding the situation created with the young lady. If you hurry, you might get to that meeting."

"Actually, I did. I hope I didn't keep you waiting for too long."

The expression on his face change from the one obtained by ingesting pickles to that of a new father of a perfectly healthy child. It seems that my approach has put him in difficulty, so before he'll tear his face muscles, I continue, "Chief Quaestor Dan Demetriad, nice to meet you." I reach across the table to greet him.

"Apetrei Mircea, Chief of Station. The pleasure is all mine!"

As the door remain open, the ones outside also heard my name. A small commotion took place behind me. A new agent of the police exclaimed, "Man! Is this Dan Dracu?"[3] Therefore, he obviously belongs to the category of people who just heard of me. There are also persons who belong to the "Dă-l Dracu"[4] category, people who have made it to my blacklist and now serve heavy years of jail, as well as those from the "Dat Dracu"[5] category, who have worked with me directly and have seen that nothing escapes me. In short, I'm double D.

"First of all, I'm here to ask for your help in a private investigation. Don't worry, it's nothing illegal. I just need data about some persons."

"What exactly are we talking about?"

"I've undertaken a private case here, so you realize I can't give you too many details. I just need the database so I can check the suspects."

"No problem, Mr. Demetriad. As long as a criminal is cornered and punished for his deed, I don't see any reason why we would not help you. Especially since the arrest will be made by law enforcement."

"I'm glad to hear this. Can you tell me from where I can access the database?"

"You can use my computer."

"Thank you."

I sit down and I log on using my data, because I have access to a higher level than most of them, and obviously I have decided to take

---

3   Dan Dracu means Dan the Devil (the original version was preferred to be used, to maintain the originality of the text) (translator's note).

4   "Send him to hell."

5   "Son of a gun" or "The one who hears the grass grow"

advantage of this. Charges of robbery, accessory to murder, bodily injury, forgery, and use of forgery were raised against Badea—of course, none with evidence, as he was the man in the shadow. I learned that Bogdan is also named Voicu, twenty-five years of age, with a few petty crimes on his records. Nothing interesting, just that my intuition didn't deceive me this time, and Cezar had been sent directly on target. Alina doesn't appear here at all; clearly her back is very well covered. Therefore, I will not look like a schmuck and a profiteer. I return to my companion.

"Can we make an official inspection of the Section? Of course, if you agree. I think a positive report on you would look nice."

"I can't see why not, come with me."

One after the other, the agents are presented to me together with their latest achievements. I love this view. It reminds me of my freshman period, when we were playing poker for pushups and stood straight for hours, because Cannon Head was coming for an inspection and banged us with a idiotic command like: "Can you see the horizon? I can't, so jog to it and return to report what you saw!" Only this time I was the Cannon Head. In the end, I request a general visual inspection, and with a sign all agents have started taking their desks by storm, papers flying everywhere, caps, tanks, rhinos, giraffes, a Boeing, four carrots, well and truly like in the Revolution. In a few minutes, they're standing aligned in front of me. I say good-bye and head for the exit, after more than four hours spent there. I get out on the street and call my recruit, who tells me that it will be a while until he finishes but that he has good news. I decide to walk among streets and thoughts. And from thought to thought I hear, "Gândul![6] Gândul, Gândul! Get Gândul!"

I raise my eyes and I see a little gipsy kid with a stack of newspapers in his hand, coming toward me.

"How much for one?"

"One RON, mister."

"Come on, give me one."

"Here you go, mister." And he pulls out a newspaper folded separately from the others.

"I will give you one RON extra if you give me today's newspaper."

"All right, mister."

---

6   Romanian newspaper named *Gândul* (meaning *"The Thought"*) (translator's note).

"Here, take this one back. Sell it to a blind man, who doesn't realize."

"I can't take it back, mister. That one I have from that man. He gave me ten RON to bring it to you, and if he sees me taking it back, he'll beat me and then take my money."

"BUM! Zbang!" Thoughts are racing inside my head and logic kicks in.

I immediately ask, "What man?" and he points at a shady looking guy sitting on a bench across the street from us,. I see him, but it's already too late. The sign the kid made toward him made him get up and foot it. I activate the propellers, enter turbo mode, drop my cigar, and break into a run toward him. The shoes and suit reduce my aerodynamicness, and my speed is reduced to half. (In truth, this is just an excuse for the fact that I don't move that quickly, even though in the fourth grade I came fifth at sprinting.) I see him entering the mall hoping to lose himself in the crowd. I come in and search for him. This is a bachelor's paradise—ladies of all ages, all colors, all species. I see him running toward the exit to the parking garage, and there I go. Running like an ogre and expectorating the last four packs of cigarettes, I reach the parking garage just in time to see him getting on a car. Just like in the movies, I see the car leaving, but the director doesn't let me see the plate number, so it's completely useless. I light up a cigar, sit on the side of the road, and begin browsing through the newspaper. Banal and useless news—Uncle Gheorghe cut his hand with a hatchet, Romeo killed himself, Juliet the same. I pass by the horoscope, write down a number from matrimonials, shed a tear at celebrations, and stop in the middle of the newspaper, where there is a scanned picture with a kid holding the same newspaper and a message.

"During the following few days you will drop the investigation. The police have been contacted only to deliver the money, which is no problem for the child's father. Otherwise we will drop the ransom, and the boy will be gone forever."

Nicely said, but my conscience doesn't let me give up that easily. I slowly head to the parking exit, with my eyes wide open in case I spot a coffee machine to balance my blood pressure. I slip the newspaper in the pocket and order a taxi to take me to the hotel, where Cezar can meet me. After an hour, dear Cezar also shows up, probably jubilating because he managed to obtain something concrete, and finds me in my room, meditating.

"Boss, you won't believe it! I did as you told me and I got to several veterinary offices."

"Well, what was the point of sending you to do something if you wouldn't have done it?"

"Yes, but at one of the offices they recognized the name and said that someone came with Rudy several times. The dog was registered there. They said it had some problems with its appetite."

"Good, so you found out that the dog kicked the bucket because of starvation? Or that he ran in the jungle searching for food?"

"They've spoken to her and told them that every time Marius left home the dog refused to eat or drink water, and that maybe they can give him some treatment to help him regain his joie de vie."

"Hey, that's good! So the dog was loyal, actually very loyal, to Marius. No wonder he started another family considering the amount of attention the child got from his parents. And we could have got this information directly from Cristina. I'm not particularly interested in the ulcer the dog might have had. Have you learned something about Bogdan?"

"Nothing special. At another clinic, they told me that he had worked there until several months ago, and then he left."

"So where does the dog food smell come from? Maybe I just imagined it, but at least I was right."

I resume my meditation in the armchair and look again at the photo found in the newspaper. Nothing that could explain the location. A big white wall, the boy dressed in a track suit and sneakers. I notice that he isn't upset at all by his posture, and there are no signs of violence, at least none visible. The phone ruins the silence. Ingrid. It's only been four days and she's already looking for me?

"How do you do. To what do I owe this pleasure?"

"Hello, Dan. Come on, stop it. It's nothing special. I'm just bored to death."

"I get it, and I am just a tool stave off boredom. Look at the bright side, you could die without me."

"In a way, you're right, I wanted to hear you. To ask you how have you been?"

"Well, thank you, just visiting. I want to open a cattle farm, and I understood Holstein are a profitable breed. Earlier I even had a coffee with fresh milk."

"Funny guy. I'm serious. How are you, when will you be back? You promised it won't take long."

"Unfortunately, my dear artist, small problems have occurred and they'll keep me here for a few more days, but don't worry, I'll look for you as soon as I return to the capital."

We jump into a long, useless discussion, full of sweet words from her. She was acting as if she found out that I'm a multi-billionaire in Russian rubles and wants to get married in a few days. Damn, where was this appetite for love of yours when I was there? Typical artists, passing from one extreme to the other so easily. Even now I have no idea what I was doing at that painting exhibition, where all the paitings looked more like smears made by elephants. She was standing there, staring at a funny mix of colors. I watched for a few minutes from behind her, trying to understand the painting's idea, then approached in a gallant fashion.

"Interesting way of transposing the infinite nature of the universe and the manner in which the author managed to eulogize the trauma though which our planet goes through, and the fact radiation is jeopardizing our health."

"Actually, here I painted a landscape using only green and red."

There goes trouble. Besides the fact that she was short and concise, she was also the author. I redressed rapidly.

"I was just being sarcastic, dear. I'm Dan!"

"Hello, I'm Ingrid."

"And this Bogdan guy is definitely involved in the dog's disappearance, and maybe he also knows something about the boy," I say to Cezar, freshly returned from the land of thoughts. Let's talk with Cristina too. Maybe we'll find out something new that could help us.

We get in the SUV and leave for Badea's house. Once we get there, we try to go in, but the gorillas at the door have a different point of view. Only after we wave our identification cards do they remember me and that I'm unstoppable. We find Cristina restlessly channel surfing, without even taking the time to see the logos of channels. She gets up and greets us with a fake smile, inviting us to a coffee. Passing over greetings and formalities, we sit down at the table and discuss.

"Regarding the boy, we received this today in an interesting manner,"

I say while throwing the boy's picture on the table. She takes it, and I can see her eyes become worried.

"I hope he's all right."

"By his looks in the picture, he's rather lively and neat. He'll probably be returned in working condition."

"Yes, probably.

"Do you recognize the landscape, any details?"

"No, just the clothing. He was dressed like this when he left."

"Considering the picture was taken the day he went missing, I think it has not been that long since the disappearance. Besides this photo, there was a note telling me that they'll contact me to deliver the money. So we'll have to wait until things settle down. I also want to ask you whether Rudy had any distinctive marks?"

"Yes, on his rear thigh he had an area with white hair. On the inside. But don't you think that Marius is more important now than Rudy?"

"You're right. Anyway, the essential thing is to recover Marius alive, and further on we'll see. I must admit, with each passing day, the chances of finding him alive are lower and lower. But for the moment I try to cling to anything that get me to Marius."

At this, Cristina's worry deepens. It's a shame to waste such a moment. Marius was practicing boxing. This is already known. Then why didn't he fight back when he was kidnapped?

Probably his reproduction instinct got a hold of it. I'm talking about Rudy, not Marius, don't get me wrong. Thoughts come to me chaotically and disorganized. It's possible that the dog's disappearance is connected to the boy. Maybe they tried abducting him from home and the dog was getting in the way. Or maybe it's just a coincidence. But since there are no other leads for the moment, there's no point in wasting time. I lift my eyes to Cristina, who was still gazing.

"We have to be leaving."

"All right. If you need anything else, call me or contact Mihai."

"Don't worry, if I can say that, we'll manage. I apologize for the sudden departure. We have to get to the Inspectorate, but we'll return." I get up and signal Cezar to follow me.

When we get to the car, Cezar seems perplexed.

"Why are we going to the Inspectorate?"

"Actually, Cezar, we're going to the dog pound to search for Rudy, but since the dog may be connected to the kidnapping, we give no such details to those involved. As you can see, we give them only the information that doesn't bring us other information. Everyone lies; you can trust nobody."

"You're right, boss."

"I always am, Cezar. I always am ..."

At the edge of the city, we find the animal shelter, a cross between a camp and a slaughterhouse. The landscape is made of garbage pilled eveywhere , overcrowded cages filled with feces and rusted wire fences, some of the cages bearing the marks of violence. A mess. We enter the building and I approach the first who comes in my way, a withered old man with clothes of different colors and sizes but all with a shade of gray. He has a grayish beard to match, full of all sorts of residues, a few missing teeth, and a stench of cheap alcohol. He is definitely a secret collaborator of city hall, sent to infiltrate the dogs, and this was only a disguise, so he would not raise suspicion among the dogs, enabling him to arrest and impound them.

"Greetings! How's it working?"

Baffled but cheerful he answers, "It works, Chief, it works. We make enough to live. Today I brought six mutts and I got some money for food for a few days. The mayor pays poorly, but what can we do? We make a living. We also bring corpses and because we clean the streets, they pay us some money for them. But I don't bring those from my cottage, because they protect me and no one comes near me. They don't eat much. I throw them a piece of bread ... to live ..."

Could Rudy be alive? My instinct tells me to ask where corpses are kept in the first place. God, I feel so dizzy! Returning to reality, the old man is still mumbling that life is hard and so on. Regretfully, I feel obliged to interrupt his eulogy, and so the alcohol vapors stop from violating my privacy causing me dizziness. You could kill someone just by talking to him. Now that's a biologic weapon!

"Yes, you're right. Still, can you tell me where can I find someone who works with papers around here?"

"Further back a bit, in that room, is Costel. He pays us."

"Long live you, dear Herodot! If it's no bother, we'll go to speak with him. Fruitful hunting!"

I slowly head for the closet called a room where Costel sits and listens quietly to the radio. You could still hear in the background the old man's greetings, but my eyes are fixed on my new interlocutor.

"Greetings, Mr. Costel."

"My regards. How may I help you?"

"Well … I'm looking to get a dog. Can I take it from here?"

"Of course, people sometimes come to get one, just like that. You just need to fill in this form."

"Good. To spare some time, I'm interested in one that doesn't eat much, maybe nothing even, which doesn't make a mess, doesn't bark, and is nice and stiff."

"Well, that would mean getting a dead dog!"

"Perfect! Do you know where the corpses are being kept?"

"Hey, are you making fun of me?"

"No, but I don't want to lose any time." I throw my identification card under his nose. I'm looking for a missing dog, which is very likely to be dead.

"Come with me. They're here in the back," he babbles through tobacco-stained teeth.

We make a short slalom between cages and sacks of food before coming to a covered container.

"We're not allowed to keep them here for more than two days, for hygiene reasons, so the guys from Environment come and take them and incinerate them.

I look at them while our dear Cezar resultfully disgorges, leaning against the building. Only stray. Nothing interesting.

"We're looking for a Rottweiler, but it seems we're not lucky. Do you have any among the living animals?"

"No, but we had a Rottweiler a few days ago, brought by some boys from a clinic. They said they had found him on the street, but wasn't dead yet, so they tried to help him. They didn't succeed, so they brought him here."

"Do you have their phone number?"

"Of course, we keep records of all veterinary clinics. We sometimes collaborate with them. I have it written in my agenda. Come with me."

Back in his "office," he fumbles though an agenda that's probably as old as he is. Among hieroglyphics he stops on a string of numbers.

"There it is! VetLab. Mister … I don't understand his name, but this is the phone number."

"Thank you for your help! Maybe next time we'll be luckier in finding a dog to my liking."

"I advise you to get a turtle. It's the perfect animal."

"I can't. She will be just a true young lady when I'll die so I don't want to hurt her feelings."

I write down the number and we say good-bye to him, as well as to Plato, who seems to be carefully planning his next move, while trying to maintain his balance. We try our luck, even though since it's after 5 p.m. we don't expect that anyone will be there. It seems that this time we're lucky, as there is someone is at the other end of the line, but he says that they're just leaving, and if there's no emergency we could meet the next day. This situation doesn't bother me at all, so we schedule for a "consultation" the next day. On our way, we stop to have a coffee while Cezar is making his last notes—or drawing rhinos on his notebook. Whichever, at least it keeps him busy.

We go back to the hotel, where he fills his stomach with food while I peacefully enjoy my coffee.

"Tonight we'll make another visit to Alina's club. Maybe we'll learn something else …" I think out loud.

"Have you already spoken to her?" He answers in between bites.

"Yes, I told her to prepare a lamb stake in the oven."

"And what can I do, boss? I already ate."

"You amaze me, Cezar. You should lighten up. No, I haven't spoken to her, because it's not connected to the investigation. We're going out for fun."

Around ten we leave from the hotel, headed toward Arcade. Honestly, I was hoping that we wouldn't find Alina there, so we could unwind at ease. This time I also take Cezar, who is still horrified by those corpses, and he might as well return the food he had a little earlier. Probably those images affected his brain, because he dressed like an unemployed Santa Claus.

To my surprise, like yesterday, the club is almost empty—only a few tables with night wanderers and two to three tables that have not yet been cleaned up, but a simple calculation of the prices of products show that cleaning them is not worth it.

The same girl as last time comes toward me. She either has a good visual memory or I am extremely charming, because she approaches me straight away, holding two menus.

"Nice to see you again," I offer before she can say anything.

"Welcome back," she replies while handing me the menu.

"Thank you. I'd like a coffee and a bottle of red wine, demi-sec, preferably from '99. The drought of that year blessed the wine with a distinguished intenseness. And a glass. And an ashtray. And ten minutes of your life. And a Coke for him."

"There is still a small problem. I don't think I can offer you the minutes of my life."

"I'll accept hours, if needed. I'll give you change."

We smile to each other, and she vanishes in the dark to get our order.

Sipping from the glass of wine, I try to connect things in my mind, and Cezar dearly hums the songs playing in the club. Finally, an activity for his taste.

But what is his taste? Arsenic? Cyanide? I don't think so. These are a bit too violent. If my suspicions are correct, Bogdan tried different poisons on dogs from the clinic in a desperate attempt to get rid of Rudy, which would have stood in his way in the case of a kidnapping, because it would have followed Marius. And even so, a week before? Something doesn't add up. And after he got rid of the dog, how did he kidnap the boy without Alina noticing? Or is she also involved? I don't think so; she cared too much for him. Or is that only a façade? Could Cristina be involved? If so, she would have to be a very good actress, because one could clearly see in her eyes that she cares. And what debts or dubious business does Mihai have that it would come to this? This sounds either like revenge or stupidity on the part of the abductors. It would have been much easier to eliminate him. I didn't manage to get at least one name from Mihai. He won't give them to me even if it's the last thing he does, it's clear. I take a break and signal the girl to come.

"What else can I get for you?

"Your presence," I say, using my wonder-working ID card. I'll ask to be buried with it. Maybe I can use it with St. Peter when I'll reach heaven's gates. But with what I have done so far, I think I won't see those gates even in pictures, but at least I'll be chief in the boiler room, in hell.

"Have a seat, please."

"You know I can't sit at the table with a client during work."

"Then we can go in the back! My God, I love this line. Don't worry, I'm here on business. If needed, I can write you a hand-written excuse."

"Fine, wait until I notify my colleagues that I'll be missing, and we can go."

She returns to the bar and signals me to follow her. Once we get in the back, I waft her to sit down on the chair I had found piled among other useless things gathered from inside . I mix this psychological advantage I have obtained with a tough, firm attitude and start the discussion, going around in circles so as not to draw suspicion.

"Good, who takes care of the club?"

"Well, the club belongs to Miss Gruia."

"Gruia?"

"I suppose you know her as Alina."

"Yes, that's right."

Gruia, Gruia, where have I heard this name before? Gruia ...

"So it belongs to her, but who runs it?"

"Miss Gruia."

"Nobody else? I've seen she's somewhat busy ..."

"That's right, but also Miss Gruia takes care of it."

It seems I've blocked her on only one answer. I exaggerated a bit, so I try to mend the situation.

"What time do you and your colleagues finish work?"

"We have to stay until the last customer leaves."

"And you all stay for only one client?"

"What do you mean by that?"

"That maybe we could leave together earlier, to drink a glass of wine at the hotel. I have an old bottle, since about four hours ago. That too was a good crop, you know."

"Your invitation is rather sudden. Are you using your position to take advantage of me? No, I will not come. If you want, we can talk here."

"Our discussion here is finished. I will not use my position, and if you won't come, it's all right. You don't have to agree with me, but it's easier this way."

"Easier to do what?"

"To realize that you consider me nice and that you're curious."

"Curious about what?"

The girl plays tough and seasons her lines with various alluring female gestures. Now's the moment to act.

"Nothing. Thank you for your help."

I smile to her and turn around to leave. As I expected, she continues.

"But I have to get home before 3 a.m."

"That's perfect. Tonight I was planning to clean my room anyway."

"Fine, I'll talk to the others to see what I can do," she says smiling.

We leave the storage room and I go to our table, where Cezar dances like a seal in a desperate attempt to mate. I quietly finish my bottle of wine, look around the club, and then get up and head straight toward her.

"There are only two customers left. Do you think your colleagues can manage without you?"

She smiles and grabs my arm, signaling them that she's leaving. Cezar also gets up and drives us safely to the hotel room. There I cling to a bottle of wine from the minibar while she's looking around the room. In the club, because of the weak light, I didn't manage to discern her facial features. But now, in the room's light, I can see her much more clearly, and I wonder why I haven't invited her anywhere since last time. She isn't particularly tall, but she's well built. She looks exactly like an hour glass, and her blond hair is the sand slowly pouring down her back, up to her round and savory bottom. My eyes have managed to go through her bra, seeing breasts shaped like freshly ripened green apples. What a pity …

After some wine, the girl is sufficiently cheerful. I sit on the bed in front of her, disrobe her with my eyes, and tell myself, "Come on, you can do it! I know you can do it!" And I can. I manage to suppress my wild outbursts in front of the seventeen-year-old girl and to start a conversation.

"Why is a girl like you working in a club? Isn't it a bit dangerous?"

"Actually, not at all. I do this for money."

"What a thing. I was thinking that you do it to learn more about endangered animals. And is it worth it?"

"At first it was, but now sales are low, and if there are no sales, there are no tips …"

"And why don't you leave?"

"Because I like it."

"I like penguins, but that doesn't mean that I'll move to a glacier. There are so many things you could do without losing your nights."

"I have one year until I finish high school, and after …"

"After what? If you've got the taste of lost nights since now, even finishing high school is uncertain. If you become an eagle, you'll eat corpses your whole life. You'll never be able to be a Hummingbird."

"But I could be a phoenix."

"It's just a myth. Things that burn remain ash."

She comes near me and starts caressing my belly. This isn't allowed. I grab her gently by the hand and I create a diversion by leaning over her a bit and kissing her. I can't believe I'm doing this. My conscience slaps me. "You idiot! She's seventeen!" "You're right, conscience, but it's clear that the girl is no beginner." "And what, do you want to take advantage of that?" "Hmm, no … I was just saying …" "If you touch her, I'll hunt you your entire life!" "You'll do that anyway." The discussion with myself manages to calm me down so I can resume the subject.

"And how come it's not working anymore?"

"Alina started taking from the supply money for I don't know what—businesses that didn't work—and that's why we reduced our stock, until clients had nothing left to buy. Most of them went elsewhere."

"How well do you know Alina?"

"I've know her for a year or so. She's a profiteering bitch, and she would sell her soul for money …"

She pushes against me and knocks me on my back, and now she's standing on top of me. Profiteering bitch? This sounds like envy.

"And what is Bogdan doing at the club? I've seen him in front of the bar buried in papers."

"He's the one helping Alina with everything, desperately trying to solve the problem."

"Then why doesn't she borrow money from Badea again?"

"She already did. She asked him to return all the money that Badea initially invested in the club, and a bit more. And now she doesn't want to return it."

"The truth is that a player returns to the casino not because he's winning, but because he's losing. How do you know that she doesn't want to give the money back?"

"I don't know, I just assumed. Anyway, I don't care."

Excellent, too much wine. Now everything she says doesn't make sense, or these are just her drunken doll thoughts.

Oh, Dear Mother! The drunken doll has just taken off her shirt, and I must admit that this sight is even rarer than a total eclipse of the sun. This time I cannot bear it anymore. I slowly pull myself from under her, hug her, and whisper in her ear, "Here's my phone number. Call me in a few years!"

It is difficult to describe her reaction. On a scale from one to ten, hurricanes are a three, and she's a nine. The flood in the Bible is like a summer rain. Lucky I drank alcohol, which allowed me to endure everything without even shedding a tear. I could have opened a zoo if I had all animals she likened me to.

She got dressed and left. Deep down, I knew I had done the right thing, and I was going to continue doing the right thing, a cold shower!

My morning coffee finds me in the same armchair, only this time the room looks a bit worse than yesterday, glass everywhere and a massive jaw ache. I gapingly observe that one of my eyes won't open. Yes, now I remember! She slapped me! That's where all the glass came from. By sheer coincidence the hand she used to slap me was holding one of the wine bottles. It seems that I got her really, really angry. But it's all right—the important thing is to remain focused on the investigation. I also brief Cezar, who is paying more attention to the chaos in the room than to what I am saying.

"Yes, Cezar, she's a little beast. Stay away from her. I still need you. And I think her too. Let's go to the veterinarian's office; maybe we'll get lucky and adopt a pelican, so we can be a happy family."

Once we arrived at the veterinarian's office, I enter directly with my identification card in my hand, because my looks no longer help me. I managed to see my left eye in the mirror, and it's just a pink bump. A guy greets us while feeding some balloon fish. I come closer and watch the fish.

"Good morning. How can I help you?"

"Hello. We need a little help. The other day you found a poisoned dog, a Rottweiler. I'm interested in the medical sheet for his treatment."

"Yes, what a shame. It was very well cared for, didn't show signs of violence … we didn't manage to find out what killed it. Come with me."

I grab the report and start reading, and I find exactly what I was interested in.

"Distinctive marks: White spot on the inside thigh. Cause of death: poisoning, unknown substance." In the detailed analyses I find hypoglycemia and insulin shock. I immediately think of "Xylitol."

"Excuse me?" says the doctor. It seems that I have spoken out loud once again, so I move on.

"Xylitol, sweetener for us, killer for dogs. Legislation stipulates that killing pets is a felony. So, nobody can be charged with murder, you can find Xylitol in chewing gum, in vitamins. If you have the necessary equipment, you can extract it, and *voila*! You have legal poison for dogs. So even if we find the one who did this, we can only bow to him. He got rid of a damn inconvenient eye witness."

"You might be right. I'll redo the tests. I still have some samples I've saved, and I think they're enough. But how did you know about the Xylitol?"

"I had a dog with really bad mouth odor, so I gave him chewing gum. Each time he got sick, so I took him to the doctor's, and after a while they managed to figure this out."

"You did? Did he die from the same cause?"

"Yes, he became addicted, and one day he went on his own to the store where he saw me get the chewing gum."

"And the seller gave the dog the pack of chewing gum, which he ate?"

"No, halfway down the road a truck sent him to chewing gum paradise."

We thank the guy and head for the home of the Badea family. I see Alina's car parked in front of the house. Right on time. She'll definitely want to find out the news.

We go upstairs, where irritated voices are shouting.

"Alina, it's been one year. Where is the money? What happened to it? I trust you completely, and what do you do? I thought we had a deal! I hope you solve this soon, otherwise the club is mine, and don't you dare comment!"

"I'll get the money. Don't worry, things will get sorted. For now, let's solve the problem with Marius. I really am worried about him."

"I know, me too. Have you learned anything so far?"

"Unfortunately, nothing ..."

"I did."

Everyone turns toward me.

"I'm sorry to bust in like this. I asked at the entrance if it's all right to come up, and they let me."

"It's fine, Mr. Demetriad. Make yourself at home."

"Thank you! Unfortunately, I found the dog."

"Great!" says Badea falsely, trying to hide his nerves and tribulation from the earlier conversation.

"And where is it now?" Cristina asks in disappointment, seeming to guess my answer.

"Rudy is dead." I blurt this out with the intention of causing an immediate reaction. Out of the corner of my eye I watch Bogdan's reaction. He's sitting somewhere around the bar. You could tell from a mile away that his pulse was going haywire. The veins on his hands swelled to face the blood pressure. Alina has no reaction. She is staring me, long and blank, as usual.

"The dog was poisoned by someone and abandoned on the street."

"What?!"

"Did you find out who did this?" Cristina asks.

"No, and neither the poison which was administered to it."

I wasn't stupid enough to tell them everything in front of the alleged killer.

Mihai quickly moves on and replies.

"What have you found out about Marius?"

"Except for the photo we have received, and the fact that we'll be contacted, nothing. And there's something more. I cannot run the investigation of your son's disappearance anymore, some problems came up and I have to return to the capital. Honestly, I advise that you pay the ransom to recover your son—it's the safest way. Also, the police will have to be notified about the case. I'll recommend you an inspector who has dealt with such cases."

"So you're leaving us at that?" Mihai fights back.

"I'm sorry, I won't be able to help you any further. I hope things go well and that you'll solve the problem without complications. Tomorrow I'll still be in town, in case the kidnappers contact me to communicate their requirements to you. At least I can do this to help you."

I was hoping that Bogdan, hearing this, will tell the others that there is no investigation and he will keep the boy alive.

"I can't believe this! My child lays somewhere, in who knows what cellar, and the only man capable of helping me abandons me! This is incredible! There really is nothing we can do for you to stay? Is it about money? I'll pay you more—it doesn't matter, I don't care!"

"Not at all. Money is enough, but I can't stay, and please understand that I can't divulge the reason. I'd endanger the other case."

"Fine, I'll transfer you today the amount for your services so far. I hope everything gets solved."

We cleared the issue of the fee, which was, in all fairness, pretty consistent, negotiated for the dog's case. I turn around and head toward the exit. Cezar is standing put, in awe.

"Cezar, you came with me, you're leaving with me. Come already!"

"Ummm, I'm coming."

In the car he's almost crying. I am so upset to see him sad, but I leave him like this for a few good minutes while I circle around the town in search of a good restaurant to eat something healthy.

"Be patient until tomorrow, Cezar, I hope I'm right."

"What do you mean, boss?"

"Don't ask me now. I honestly don't know what to answer. It's just a hunch."

The chapter between chapters
Or the unexpected chapter

Morning, again. Coffee, again, more this time. Cezar goes out to get a few newspapers to fill our time. We're browsing through the press, but I swear that neither of us is even reading the headlines.

"Tell me, Cezar, when are you planning to get married?"

"Boss, it's hard. Dad wants me to become a good cop."

"You can be good on a twelve-hour schedule."

"Yes, boss, but look at you. You're not working a schedule. You can move anywhere, anytime. The important thing is to get the problem solved, right?"

"Yes, Cezar. I don't have a schedule because I work twenty-four-seven but learn that I haven't always been like this. When I joined the police I was married, I had a good life."

"And what happened?"

"I became obsessed with a murder, and I dedicated my every second to the case. It was the first time when I was investigating in private, because the station closed the case for lack of evidence. And I kept on pushing until I realized that my wife had packed. I tried to explain, I tried to convince her that things would be different, but only after I solved the case."

"And did she stay?"

"Yes, for about ten minutes, that's how long it took her to pack our girl's things."

"Girl? You have a child?"

"Yes, a girl. She's nine now. I'd show you a picture of her, but I don't have one. Only the phone numbers I know by heart, and I still speak to her from time to time."

"Why don't you go back, boss?"

"It's easy to say, but that would mean quitting my job too, and it's the thing I know best. I can't see myself doing anything else. This is the price to pay for my ingenuity. It sounds stupid, right? I'm already at the level where I don't check twice while backing up. Maybe I could have convinced her to stay, maybe we would have had a peaceful life further, but I couldn't. Maybe it's ego, maybe I'm just sick, but this is me. So learn what you can and get married, it's painfully hard to sleep in the armchair every night, not being able to keep your family's photo in your wallet because you are afraid of the repercussions, not having any friends, not existing so you can't get harmed."

"You're right, boss. I think I'll get married," he answers, dropping his eyes to the paper.

And silence covers the room again, in expectance of any sign from the "stars."

Coffee after coffee and thought after thought, and this is how the evening finds me, the same landscape, the same two persons, one on the side of the bed with the remote in his hand and me lying on the armchair, smoking. Not even a travel pigeon from the kidnappers. The only solution I could think of was going after Bogdan and trying to find out what happened.

Easier said than done, because we didn't have the slightest clue of where to find him, and if he is part of the abductors' gang, it's clear that he would avoid any confrontation. Lacking ideas, I called Alina and set a meeting with her the same evening, without expressly requesting that Bogdan would be present, but since he was almost always with her, I figured that he would also show up. Really stupid thought. I wind up face to face, just me and her, at a table in her club.

"Any word from the kidnappers?"

"Unfortunately, nothing. I'll stay around until they contact me, and then I'll head back. I have other things to solve."

"Maybe they'll contact Mihai directly."

"Highly unlikely. Until now they've contacted only me. I don't know why they would change tactics now."

"But why you? There are so many police officers in this country, or they could have contacted the relatives directly."

"This is another thing I don't know. I was hoping to learn the reason for that here."

"Maybe they turned to you because they knew that you would solve the case. Have you ever thought that this was kidnapping for appearances only?"

This made me think, not because she might be right, but the contrary. this be a revenge, two birds with one stone, the money for the boy and a failure on my record? This would harm my eagle eye reputation. My patience was reaching its limit, so I jump right into the subject.

"Where's Bogdan? As far as I've seen, you don't go to the toilet one without each other."

"He has to solve something, so I preferred that he stays and manages it while I'm missing."

It seems that I won't get anything solved by being a good guy, so I change my attitude and I get up.

"I hope he can take a short break. I want to talk to him as soon as possible. Let's go. I'm sure Cezar is bored alone in the car."

Surprised by my sudden reaction, she obeys without commenting, and we head to the car. On the way she calls him and they decide to meet him at his home. We get to a modest apartment at the edge of the town. The modest exterior of his home strongly contrasts with the interior endowments and comfort. From plasma TV sets and audio systems to sensored lighting and minibar. He's doing pretty well for an unemployed veterinarian. I ask the two to leave us alone, and in the sole company of my interlocutor, I start the questioning.

"Would you like a chewing gum?"

"No, thank you, I'm fine."

"I insist! It contains Xylitol, but that's not toxic for us."

He reaches and takes a blade from the pack. My offer had the effect I was counting on—a trace of panic appeared in his eyes.

"Did you know the dog of the Badea family?"

"Rudy? Yes, I used to see it all the time in the yard. I played with it sometimes. It was a good dog."

"As you know, I found it. Unfortunately, dead."

"What a pity, it happens."

"Honestly, it's doesn't happen so often that animals die of Xylitol poisoning. Only someone who has thorough knowledge about animals—let's say a veterinarian—could use this in order to get rid of an inconvenient witness. If you want to talk, start now, because if we get to the station, the treatment will be much more brutal, and we'll still find out what we're interested in."

"Talk about what?"

"I will count to five, and if when I get to three you haven't cooperated, I will handcuff you and hit you with every metallic object we find on our way to the station. And just to make it even more exciting, we'll walk."

"It was an accident."

"I believe you, you just happened to have fifty packs of gum, which the dog stole, opened and spat out after he chewed. How did you extract the Xylitol from the gum?"

"I have a friend who's a chemist. But we didn't use gum, the quantity is too small and hard to extract. We used vitamins. I don't know how he decomposed them, and I wasn't even interested, as long as I had the Xylitol concentrate."

"And how did everything happen?"

"Marius left for his training, and I poured the entire bottle in its water bowl. In half an hour it was already lethargic. I took it and left it at random in the town, to make it look like an accident."

"And why did you do that?"

"Because ..."

"Because?"

"We wanted to break in the house. And the dog could have blown our cover."

"Who is 'we'?"

"Me, Marius, and two other friends."

"Marius? Break into his own house?"

"Yes, it would have been perfect. He knew the alarm code, he knew when his folks were gone, and he knew where the money was."

"And what went wrong?"

"His father changed the alarm code, so we dropped the idea."

"Unfortunately for Rudy, it was too late. And why did he need the money? Wasn't it easier to just ask?"

"He is in very big debt. He has a passion for casinos that went from bad to worse. And he borrowed large amounts of money from some friends."

"Who does he owe money to?"

"I only know two persons, Trifon and Paraschiv."

"Are these were the ones who were with you?"

"No, those were from the guards from Arcade."

"Does that mean that Alina knew about the robbery too?"

"No, I haven't told her anything. And the people kept their silence because they were going to be paid separately for their services."

"What do you know about the kidnapping? "

"Nothing. After the robbery episode we got into a fight, and I haven't spoken to him since."

"What did you eat for lunch?"

"What?!"

"I was trying to divert from the main talk. You're too stressed. Calm down, you're young, you have your whole life ahead of you, plenty of time to spend in jail."

The answers so far are enough, even if he denies his connection to the kidnapping. I end the series of questions and I head for the door, taking Cezar as I go. Alina decides to stay, probably to question Bogdan about what he told me. I am content about what I found out, so I don't want to lose any more time with details.

After I arrive at the hotel, I start thinking again. Things had changed radically.

I start thinking out loud, in hope that Cezar will have a flash of genius and would me with anything—at least that he will understand something.

"The dog is in no way connected to the kidnapping, but neither is Marius. The kidnapping is certainly the result of debts he acquired. The circle of suspects now includes his friends. Maybe we'll manage to find out who owed money, and how much. Maybe this will take us to the kidnappers. Too many "maybes." We need something concrete, Cezar!"

I grab the phone and call the man in the shadow, who has always helped only for the adrenaline rush he gets. At least that's what he says. Each time I finish an investigation, he makes me tell him about the reasoning of the case. Even if he's still young, his ability to use a computer is superhuman. The problem occurred when he tried to use these abilities to deceive people. He used to access databases of various travel agencies and get details about clients. Benevolent, he offered to deliver them the plane tickets or reservations, of course, also cashing the equivalent value, and then he disappeared. He never exaggerated, and the frauds were rare, because the money he used to get from the victims usually lasted him a few months. His bad luck came when he tried the same scheme with a friend of mine, who called me immediately to tell me that he had contacted his travel agency to confirm the payment, and they informed him in a nonchalant manner that he had been tricked. A surveillance camera near his residence offered me the image of the criminal, but I didn't find him in the database. This didn't bother me at all, because the prints left by his shoes on the doormat contained a mixture of cement dust and yellow clay.

I headed for the residential neighborhood under construction at the edge of the city. Six of the twenty houses had been finished, but only four had already been sold. Two of them were using the Internet, and only one of the families had a son. Don't get me wrong, I don't support this type of behavior, but if I had arrested the boy, he would have served some time in jail, which would have had the same effect as a primary school that prepares pupils to attend high school. He would become a true criminal. His fear, panic, and shaking during the discussion we had then convinced me that he would never try this anymore. As a reward, he offered to help me any time I needed. In exchange I would tell him about the cases I was working on.

"Hi, are you busy?"

"For you, never. Tell me, what can I do for you?" he replies excitedly.

"I need some details about a person. I know his name is Trifon. He's from Craiova and is connected to the Mafia here."

"More than enough. I'm on it right away. Do you think he's guilty?"

"I don't just think it, I'm sure of it! Yesterday I saw him dropping a cigar stub out of his car's window. I'll go to him and force him to admit it, and then he'll have to gather all the stubs in a one-hundred-kilometer radius area, using only a tweezer! Or maybe not. I'll find out in the meantime if he did anything wrong and we'll talk afterwards."

"Meaning when? More exactly, what case are we talking about?"

"Liviu, I don't think you want to ruin the surprise. You'll find out soon, I hope. Send me a message with all details you can obtain."

"Yes, yes, yes. If you say so. I'll talk to you when you're done."

I throw the phone on the bed and lean my head on the armchair's headrest. I'm preparing to finish another day as Cezar's footsteps drift away and the sound of the door closing behind him seals the fate of the day—but not before we wish each other good night.

I get up and head toward the bathroom before I even realize what I'm doing. Too little refreshed by the cold water thrown in abundance all over my head, I glimpse her. Such a beauty! Creamy, with foam around her mouth and a subtle smile made of bubbles tenderly binding and hugging eachother. I lean toward her, her steam floods my entire face, I feel her flavor, she desires me, that's clear. I savor her quietly, and I even thank Cezar, because he knows when quietness is needed and when a thought, however senseless, is needed to break the silence.

He also finishes his coffee, and then we get ready to leave. A new day, a new destination. I had the message with all the information required. Liviu once again proved himself useful. The level of cholesterol was the only detail missing. Otherwise, I had everything there, from his last purchases, to recent invoices, all together listed in a giant e-mail. We get in the car and head for Triton's residence. We have a long drive ahead of us, as his house is located about twenty kilometers from the town.

An enormous yard, surrounded by a high concrete fence, made it look like the walls of a medieval castle. The video-intercom at the gate rings and a young lady opens and invites us into the yard. Here, the stone paved alley is fenced by lawn and various garden statues, all from the oriental culture. Once in front of the door, we face some difficulties, because there is no door knob. My first reaction is to grab Cezar and use him as a battering ram.

A voice wakes me from my sadistic thoughts, and the door opens with the push of a button. Hmm, and what if you come home hurrying to get to the toilet and you can't find the remote control to open the door? That's why I prefer the classic method with a healthy door knob. We learn that the young lady is the individual's wife and that he's not home. After exchanging some polite words, we leave, still baffled by the arrangements in the yard. The artificial pond is lit, and the fish, of different sizes and colors, make their way through decorations. What a boring life, circling in the same water with the same "pond" mates, the same food, seemingly fallen from the sky. I can't stand the thought of being a fish. I would kill myself by taking a big breath of air. Leaving aside the fact that I'm the one circling in this investigation. I grab my phone and dial the number, which is meant to bring me some information.

"Hello, Mr. Trifon?"

"Yes, who is this?"

"Demetriad, Dan Demetriad is my name. I would like to talk to you as soon as possible, if you can."

"What about?"

"I'm a private investigator, and I believe you could supply some information that would help me in an investigation."

"Hmmm ... whatever, I don't see what role I could have in the investigation of a private detective. I'm in the center of the town now, so, if you want, we can meet here to talk. Come to the park in front of City Hall."

"Thank you, I will see you there soon."

After arriving in the park, I call him again only to spot him a few meters away.

We approach him, and I reach out to greet him. He's small in stature and chubby. He has short hair, probably because his hair is curly and it would look weird if he wore it longer. Hanging diagonally over his shoulder is a fanny pack that is very thight on his huge belly. He looks like a true family man, and from the discussion we had earlier, I could tell that he is the type of man who knows what he wants and everything he does, sooner or later it comes back as a profit for him. Next to him is a little hairy thing. It looks like a lion that's been shrunken in the washing machine. A brown imperial Pekinese, with relatives among the king of the animals. Its big, and round eyes come out of the eye sockets when it starts barking, which makes him look like a hairy snail.

"What's his name?"

"Rex."

"Nice name."

"Garn, my dog and a few other thousands of canines in this country are named Rex, but you can't tell the owners it's an ugly name, because they're either your friends, or you just met them and it would be rude, or you are one of them. And ... what were you saying this is about?"

"Do you know Marius Badea?"

"Yes, I had some business with his father."

"That's it?"

"Why? I don't really understand what's going on and how I am related to this entire situation."

"Somebody informed us that Marius owed you money."

"Yes, a fairly large amount, but I don't think I'll get any money from him. He called me about two weeks ago to tell me that it would take a while but that he'll return my money with interest."

"Should I understand that he's not a reliable person?"

"No, it's not that, but he's kind of missing right now. The last time I spoke to him he told me he was in some sort of trouble."

"What kind of trouble was he talking about?"

"He said that he drove a friend's car and smashed it, so he needed some money to fix it and to give some to the police officers. Long story."

"He didn't mention anything about a casino?"

"No, never, but I did see him a couple of times at the Queen Casino, losing large amounts of money playing poker and blackjack. It's none of my business, so I stayed out of it."

"What can you tell me about a certain Paraschiv?"

"He's a friend. Unfortunately, he's in prison now, and I believe he'll be locked away for a long time."

Incredible, there's a gangster behind bars. I wonder how he blew his cover.

"What is he in for?"

"First-degree murder. I don't know many details. As far as I understood, he was caught while shopping, something about supermarket receipts. He's locked up here, at Craiova Penitentiary, if you want to talk to him."

"No, thank you, I'm horrified of bars and criminals gathered in one place. I have criminal-phobia. Anyway, if he's locked away for murder, I have all the time in the world to go visit him. Thank you for the information, and please contact me if you find out anything new about Marius."

"Of course, all the best."

We leave our companion in the care of the neurotic dog and head to nowhere at a good pace. Things are starting to shape up ... nothing more.

Chapter IV
Or the fourth

Back at the hotel, I call Mihai to explain exactly what the situation is. He's the only one I trust, because he's paying. I also tell him that there is a chance the kidnapping was staged by his own son.

"Sir, there is a problem. The kidnappers specified that I should cease my involvement with the investigation, or they will kill him. I want to stay and continue the investigation in a more discrete manner."

"Good, then we'll have to find a pretext for you to stay in Craiova."

"An assassination," I reply.

"What?! What do you mean?"

"Yes, an assassination. And in order to be able to remain in touch, the assassination will take place in one of your clubs. This will allow us to contact each other without rising any suspicions. But those around you mustn't know the real reason for my stay."

"Fine ... but how do we do that?"

"Well, that's sort of my job ... I just need a little support from you."

After I hang up, I have another short conversation on the phone, then start preparing for a walk.

It's a warm summer evening, so the formalwear I usually adopt is replaced by a casual T-shirt and a pair of three-quarter-length pants, richly decorated with pockets. Cezar also dresses in a comfortable outfit, and we leave in search for a refuge for the rest of the evening. After walking by several clubs, I decide on one, coincidently or not belonging to Mihai.

"Tell me, Cezar, shall we pay a visit to your wife?"

"But boss, I'm not married, you know that!"

"Perhaps not, but if we search throughout history ..." and my eyes rise to the name of the club. *Cleopatra.*

Lots of cars parked outside, most of them luxury cars. The guards posted at the entrances, more than twenty I've seen so far, are nondescript; I don't think I could distinguish more than three of their faces despite my experience. They all look like closets with double gliding doors, wearing sunglasses in summer, winter, light, or total darkness, and on some of them you could observe an earplug coming down their back neck, as if they were plugged in to stay loaded at all times. We climb the stairs and one of them greets me, nodding.

Inside it is so crowded that I thought each car brought six people. It is crowded and uncomfortable, but we manage to sneak over to the bar, where I confiscate two chairs. We order a beer each and we admire the landscape. Maybe I'll manage to relax a bit and purify my physique, using only the power of mind and a young lady around here. Scanning the area in search of prey, I can't see anything, so I start a conversation with the young lady from the bar, taking advantage of the background noise.

"Yes, we could try, but don't you think it's too crowded here?"

"What?!" she replies as she leans over the bar, trying to understand what I'm saying.

"It's too noisy in here! We'll go outside after you finish your job!"

"What makes you think that I will go with you ..."

"Because I can't see why not, when actually we both want to."

"Interesting way of putting it. This time ..."

The rest is lost in the immense space of the universe, because Cezar grasped me from the moment's quietness to show me that somewhere in the corner a fight had started. It started with only a few gestures, but things go crazy and people step back, forming a circle around the four persons pulling caps. Someone screams, frightened, "He stabbed him!"

I get up from the bar and go toward that location. Some have come to see what happened, while others left for the exit. There is total chaos, screams, the whole deal.

I approach the victim and I see a pool of blood. You could already hear sirens from outside, and a few police officers entered the club, starting to evacuate the ones inside. One of the policemen comes close and leans over the victim.

"Is he dead?" I ask.

"No!" the police officer answers while standing over him. "Quickly, call an ambulance!"

"What ambulance? Can't you see he's bleeding like a pig? Get him in my car and I'll take him to the hospital. Come on, quickly!"

After laying him on the backseat, I flounce off. Soon the club is out of the sight of my review mirror, and the sound of sirens fade. I change the lane and head for another direction. Cezar turns to me.

"Boss, why are we heading for the park?"

"To have another beer there. I heard the summer stars look nice from the park."

"And what if he dies?"

"Who? The pig is dead anyway!"

"That cop said he's still breathing and you said we're taking him to the hospital."

"I see nothing escapes you. There's a risk of dying, but only if he slips into an alcoholic coma." I turn my neck toward the backseat and, lifting my hand in sign of wonder, draw a cross in the air and give an order.

"Get up and walk, Lazarus!"

A shadow rises off the backseat. The headlights of cars passing by us light up his face. He leans and searches under my seat, pulling out a can of beer.

"These guys from the Purgatory have nothing to quench my thirst in the waiting room."

"Purgatory is for those who still have a chance of reaching heaven! Anyway, I loved the way you did it—it seemed like you had your throat slashed."

"I did good, didn't I?" And he starts laughing. We're both laughing aloud while Cezar is trying to get his breathing back

"Cezar, say hello to my friend, Valentin, colleague of mine from the Academy and a failure in life. How's your sister?"

"She's fine, healthy. I hope I get to meet her one day."

"Boss, isn't he that guy?"

"Yes, he is. I'm surprised you didn't realize it earlier. Such a look can't be easily forgotten. He's the one I looked for today, asking him to get a few kilos of blood from a slaughterhouse so we could frame an assassination. The police will take statements from witnesses who saw a dead man, and they'll find out from me that he simply fainted from fear when he felt the touch of a knife, and that'll be enough to stop looking for a body. Then will have a phantom assassination who will be investigated only by myself."

"Don't listen to him, son. If you listen to Dan you'll end up dying on your feet. Look at me! And since we're talking about me, I have been notified by my brain that I need some food."

"No problem, I have a crossbow in my trunk. You'll be able to hunt in the park. If you have no luck, we can order a pizza anytime."

"Maybe for you, I'd rather rent a whole restaurant and enjoy myself."

We spend the rest of our evening in different restaurants and bars, where my friend eats any type of food available, whether hot or cold, fresh or prepared over the day. He seems not to be interested even if the food is still alive when it reaches his stomach. In the morning we take him to the train station, and he boarded on the first train, literally the first train in the station, heading somewhere north.

The next day (for those who lost the hours of the night, sleeping, as for us it was just a continuation of the previous day) finds me in the armchair savoring a cup of coffee. Since my brain was demanding the dose of caffeine more and more insistently, I unpacked the cup I always carry with me. It's old and loaded with memories. Physically, it's banal, a simple cup without decorative elements, drawings, or paintings, of a used yellow color, and the interior is lined by small cracks of the enamel, which over the years have thickened so they look like a mosaic. Physically he has the capacity of two café lungo, which spares my time between two refills. It has been by my side during the most difficult moments—when my daughter was born, when the revision of the central heating in my apartment was performed, it even assisted a few love scenes watching silently from the nightstand.

Now the table is empty, and I'm standing ready to leave. Cezar sleeps like a koala after a large feeding of eucalyptus, so I leave him at peace and leave on my own to Badea's house to inform them about the "assassination." Under any circumstances, Badea had to bring at his house both Alina and Bogdan, the couple of the year, which I would suggestively name tiller-winch. Why? Because they're always together and apparently they don't function properly one without the other. I can tell that the winch can't move without the tiller but in the same time, in this couple there is no affection. Returning to the tiller, also simply known as Bogdan, I do not trust him at all and I'm not fully convinced that he's not connected to the kidnapping. I hope I can make some connections tonight. I reach Badea's house and inside I find only him. He's relaxing over a glass of vodka, doing absolutely nothing.

"As you know, last night someone was stabbed in the Cleopatra club, which belongs to you, and unfortunately the person died on the way to the hospital. Let's drink to him!"

The man seems outraged and takes his role seriously, leaving the impression that he wanted to become an actor and this is the peak of his career.

In a few minutes, Cristina enters the room very agitated, together with Alina and Bogdan.

"What happened? I understood that a fight took place at Cleopatra last night."

"Yes, and a guy died," Mihai said, blank, sitting at the bar with a glass in his hand.

Cristina sits on the couch, thinking that not even she knew the truth. But it was all for the best.

"Yes, Miss, unfortunately it's true."

"It seems we're cursed," says Mihai, taking a big sip of vodka.

Silence covers the entire room. Nobody is saying anything, and everybody is staring away. I take advantage of this opportunity to resume everything in my head. From the dog to the child and everything around. The circle of suspects is really small. Actually all I have to do is to find something that links Bogdan to the disappearance. Or maybe even Trifon. But how? Bogdan denied it, and he certainly will not blow his cover. Killing a dog is one thing, but to be on the list of kidnappers is much more serious. If I get him drunk and try to sleep with him he'll refuse, because we're of the same sex. To allure him with money would be useless, because if he's involved, he'll be filthy rich. Weird, something's already filthy. If Alina took him to the train station, she might be the last one who saw him before he was kidnapped. Could she be an accomplice? Trifon seems all right, maybe too alright for this situation. I wonder, when Marius called him to defer the payment, didn't he get annoyed by this and packed Marius for safe keeping? I'm only relating to hypotheses and suppositions, and it's already becoming tiring. I break the silence and stand up.

"I left a coffee cup on the bar last time."

"Empty," responds Cristina, absent.

"I wouldn't have left it if it were full."

While we are talking, I have already gotten in front of the ambrosia dispenser. I grab a cup and carefully place inside it a sufficient amount of coffee, so that it will not overflow. Still, silence all around. Mihai was relaxed, but one could read in Cristina's eyes the fury . She looks like she's about to jump and scream out loud "why me?!" Alina was so indifferent that she seemed bored, and Bogdan looked like Bogdan. Just a small piece of brain in his head but enough to do the dirty jobs. He's a true pet, ready to roll through the grass on his owner's request. He's scared about the fact that I could rat him to Mihai about Rudy, and that wouldn't really be good for his body, which would suffer so many mechanical shocks from Mihai that, in the end, he would look like a painting of Picasso. Those from the emergency room would have to assemble him like a 3D puzzle before finding out which of the holes they found is the proper one for resuscitation. He probably wonders why I don't say anything about what we discussed. Probably Alina askes herself the same question. Maybe I ask myself too why I don't do it, but for now I consider this a bonus I could use when needed, if it would ever be the case.

"And what happens now? It's not like we murdered him," says Alina, looking at me.

"No, there will be an investigation of the club to determine if the law regarding club security was observed, and then we'll search for the murderer."

"We?"

"Yes, Alina, we. Meaning myself and them, namely Dan Demetriad and the police. Who knows, maybe in the meantime Marius will show up. I'd like to meet him. About that, I recommend that you notify the police on this matter. Already the situation is out of control, and since I'm not on the case anymore, you can't leave him in the hands of destiny."

"Are you sure this is a solution?" replies again Alina.

"Of course," I answer, looking like a true idiot.

"It's absurd! They clearly specified that the police should not be contacted, in order to avoid complications. I think we should wait."

"We could wait awhile. Anyway, if he is to be gone, he's gone, so I think we shouldn't force our luck, they'll might kill him," says Mihai.

"As you wish. I'm no longer in charge of the investigation. Now the problem is in your hands. I have to leave. I have to collect evidence from the club."

I get in the car resembling a money grater, which, honestly, is starting to make a big hole in my pocket. Luckily, I'll be able to put it on the expenses sheet of the station. I don't think it will stand out between two packs of coffee, five napkins, a thousand disposable cups, a per diem SUV, and gas for an entire auto park. I head for the a sports shop and purchase a pair of basketball shoes, shorts and a few T-shirts. I race to the hotel and get Cezar, who has been browsing the TV and, dressed in my new equipment, we head for a basketball court near the boxing gym. Fortunately, a few kids are gathered there, playing and cursing. We approach them and butt in.

"Hey, guys, do you have room for one more?"

"Yo, Andi, your grandpa's here!"

They start giggling and laughing. I reply, discouraging them.

"If you don't stop, I'll tell each and every one of you when you were born, what is your mother name and why you should call me "father"! If you're so good, let's make a bet. I'll bet you ten lei that any two of you won't defeat us, me and the boy in the suit."

They laugh, especially when they see Cezar, with his nicely polished shoes and tie, looking like a piece of art to put on a shelf. They talk over it and two of them come on to the court. They seem like "veteran" players, even if they are only about eighteen.

They look like they are cut from an NBA magazine. Basketball jerseys with large numbers over simple white T-shirts, large shorts and very neat basketball sneakers. They look almost as good as me.

"Cezar, do you see that semi-circle? You stay there nicely, and if you move, don't cross the line. I'll pass to you and you return it. It's not that complicated!"

It feels like the good old days, when instead of coffee in the morning I would play a basketball game. The game starts, and people are on the sideline cheering. Cezar succeeds in standing in my way more than I was expecting, and my blocks work wonders, as gracious as kidney failures, but to be honest, I am having serious problems finishing. Things are all like plain sailing. Only three points separate us. And they score, and then we score, and so on until we realize the final score is actually eleven to one for them. Honestly, I wasn't that interested in the score. The important thing is that during the game several guys from the boxing club gathered on the side, more curious about the boy in suit who was standing put. All eyes are on Cezar, I managed to get lost in the crowd.

"Nice match, boys!" I reach in my pocket to get the money.

"There's no need. We play for pleasure. Don't sweat it."

Another team replaces us, and we sit down on the side with those who remain.

"Passes, more passes. Don't hold him. Can't you see how tall he is? Take it with a roll-out!"

I turn my eyes to the others.

"Aren't you playing?"

"We have no business with basketball. We're boxing."

"That's good too, but when you're fifty will you be able to hold a spoon in your hand?"

"It's the coolest sport, being there in the ring with someone. You dodge, hit with your left, and *bang*! A straight right and he's down!"

"I know, I have a friend who boxes. He's now training for the tournament in Sibiu in September."

"We're also training hard for the tournament now. We train twice a day."

"And aren't you going to the training camp?"

"What training camp? They don't have money to send us. There are no sponsors, and the money we're getting is from previous tournaments we've won, and we prefer to use the money to buy new equipment and train properly rather than leave for a week in a training camp and then return to fight and train using rags ... Maybe their club can afford to send them."

"He's from here, from Craiova. He left for the training camp a couple of days ago."

"Maybe the guy is a bit insane! Who knows where he needed to go and he lied to you."

"He didn't lie to me, but he lied to his old man."

"Hey, what's his name?"

"Badea. Marius Badea."

"Do you know Marius? Badea's son?"

"No, I know Badea, Marius's dad."

"He stopped showing up for training. What did I tell you; he wandered off somewhere, and his old man wasn't supposed to find out."

"All possible."

Target acquired. I got about everything I wanted to know, so I scream again to the guys in the field as if I am interested what's going on out there, and then I get up to leave.

"Guys, I'm going to leave. I still have some things to do today, and I'm running a little late. Maybe I'll see you around here." We salute each other like true sportsmen.

"Look, we didn't lose time for nothing, Cezar. Now if we find out who coined the idea of leaving for the training camp, we find out who kidnapped him, or at least that person is an accomplice."

On our way to the shed, I contact Mihai to receive some answers .

"Hello, Mihai, can you talk?"

"Yes, I'm alone. What happened?"

"I wanted to ask how you learned about the training camp."

"From Marius, of course."

This man has an extremely perceptive faculty of the obvious.

"Just?"

"Yes. Still, it's possible that Alina knows something about this."

Cezar heard the discussion and intervened.

"You can call and speak to her!"

Amazingly, another genius is here with me. I throw him a very puzzled look.

"I will!" I answer, very convinced.

"Tonight she left for Greece, for a medical conference for students. I spoke to her a few minutes ago. She called me to tell me that everything is all right there," Mihai says.

"No problem, boss. You can dial with prefix," Cezar said, very proud of his reasoning. His brilliant mind becomes more and more obvious. If I don't jump out of the car soon I feel I'll go crazy and I'll start taking notes off the prospects of condom boxes to improve my knowledge.

I hang up on Badea to dial Alina's number just to find out from a robot that her phone is turned off. Or at least this I what I suspected, not knowing a word of Greek. The robot might as well be giving me a recipe for sautéed mushrooms, so I have to rely on my intuition.

*(Asterisk)
Because it would be too much for another chapter

The kidnappers haven't called in a very long time already. Almost two weeks have passed since the disappearance. Something has happened, hopefully nothing bad.

I'm still in Craiova, due to the investigation relating to the assassination that took place in the club. No one is asking anything about it. It seems they are happy as long as no dead body shows up floating somewhere in a lake. I would call this a vacation, but there is still that stress about the poor boy who is waiting for his rescue from who-knows-what hellhole. All boredom lasts, as Cezar would say, until it ends. And he's not wrong, because one day the phone on the table rings loudly. My first reaction is to smack it in the head with my coffee mug. But it has no head. I stopped with my mug in the air and answered indolently.

"Yeah …"

"Dan?"

"Yeah …"

"Mihai. They called me about Marius. They said I should call you and get you here."

Said and done. In less than ten minutes I was in front of the hotel, with the car's pedals under my feet. I step on them and we fly off to the nest. Now, all five of us are standing in the room, waiting for the phone to ring again.

After a few minutes, Marius answers, agitated, breaking the silence.

"Hello! Yes, just a second!" He gives the phone to me.

"Do you have the money?"

"I don't, but his dad, who's present here, does."

"Good, put it in a briefcase, take a garbage bag, and come to the train station. The phone stays with you. And come alone!"

"Fine." From previous experience I know there's no point making a fuss with the police in such moments. And since so far I have told them nothing, their first question would be why they were not notified at the beginning about it, and this is how you lose precious time. And you also double the chance for that person to come home in a box. So we do as they say. Probably there is someone watching me, because as soon as I get to the train station, the phone starts ringing.

"Go and buy a ticket to Segarcea, on the next express train."

"Okay, I'll buy a ticket, but be advised that I'll discount it from your money."

"Funny guy."

"Is this an affirmation or a hunch? I want to be sure that Marius is alive. Call the house of the Badea family, and after Mihai confirms he has spoken to the boy, call me."

It takes only a few minutes until I get confirmation that Marius is safe.

"Satisfied? Now get on the train and wait for new instructions."

"Okay."

I get on the train and wait for it to leave. After another ten minutes, the phone rings again.

"Put the briefcase in the garbage bag and tie it firmly."

"Done."

"Throw the briefcase out the window."

"Are you sure?"

"Throw it now! The boy will get to you as soon as possible."

I didn't have anything to do, so I follow the instructions, throw the briefcase out the window, and I noticed that we're on a bridge and the Jiu river is flowing under us. A big splash and the bag disappears , only to emerge at the surface and float down the river.

At Segarcea, Cezar was already waiting for me at the train station. The road back seemed endless, and we still didn't get any sign from Mihai or Marius. My worst fears were now taking shape.

Now we're waiting in the hotel room. It would take a little over an hour for my suspicions to become true. The kidnappers have called and said that Marius had an accident and will not be able to get home until he gets well. I throw my phone against the wall and curse so violently that even a dead body would wake up and leave the room just to get rid of me. Cezar is turning into a ghost and his eyes grow so big that at some point I have the feeling it will pop out of his head. I guess I really freaked him out. "This is exactly why I left the impression that I dropped the investigation, Cezar, because the kidnappers know me. They know that reasoning comes before animus and that I would stop if that meant keeping Marius alive! And I had hoped this entire time that Marius didn't know that Bogdan is involved."

"Bogdan is involved?"

"Yes! Yes! At first they tried robbing Mihai, and they killed the dog so that it didn't stand in their way. They didn't want to risk getting caught because of the mutt but because Badea had changed the security code, they failed so they came with the idea to kidnapped him. Or …"

"And why didn't we arrest him, boss?"

"Yes, Cezar, arrest him for what? Peeing on the street? Throwing gum on the sidewalk? All for nothing. He wouldn't have said anything, and Marius would have died. If Marius couldn't recognize any of the kidnappers, they would have let him go after getting the money. But like this they'd risk too much. Even if Marius swore that he would say nothing, Bogdan wouldn't leave him alive. This accident is not an accident at all. It's probably a gun discharged in the back of his head, this is the accident! Get dressed, we're going to Badea's house!"

On our way, none of us said one word. Getting there, we find Mihai holding a glass of vodka.

"When they told you about the accident, could you still talk to Marius?"

"No, they said he was on his way to the hospital."

"I'm sorry to say this, but I think you already know that Marius…"

"Yes, I know, but I still hope that, miraculously, those guys are right and he'll get back home."

"I … will keep searching. Your side of the deal was honored."

"And what are you going to do?"

"I'll—"

"No, it's better if you don't tell me. Do what you have to do so that Marius gets back home, alive, or …"

The glass of vodka hits the wall in one piece and turns into shatters before hitting the floor.

Chapter V
Or chapter "vee"

For those who opened the book at random and it happened that they got exactly here, let's recap what we have so far.

Dog: missing, found dead by a very ingenious method, a sign that the author isn't an idiot, so he makes things lively for us. We know who did it, it's Bogdan, Alina's right hand and the primary suspect in the abduction, but we have no evidence. And he has the air of an idiot. The boy, Marius, missing while being taken to the train by Alina, leaving in a fictional training camp, invented by him for … this we don't know yet, and this isn't connected to anything. Ransom paid, but the boy is still missing. My main suspicion is that he found out who the kidnappers are and since one of them was close to him, or known by him, he couldn't be left alive.

We have the father, loaded with cash. Money made from petrol and through different clubs. The fact that his son was kidnapped doesn't make him panic, so he expected this, sooner or later.

We also have a stepmother. Speaks little and doesn't externalize much. She was never in the circle of suspects, but it is possible that she is an accomplice, even if there is no reason we know.

We have Alina, the girl raised and walled in money, by Mihai. Mihai, who is now asking for his share back, according to the contract. Maybe she is on the suspect list, as she clearly needs money to put her businesses in order. There are the two who Marius owed money to, Trifon the Careless and Paraschiv the Inmate.

We also have Cezar, the boy who I hope will bring me the inspiration I need to unlock this mystery. He's not doing well at his job, and he is very clumsy, besides the fact that intelligence isn't one of his best attributes. Honestly, I think someone is trying to test my resistance to stupidity, but I'm doing fine.

As a whole, we have a soup of people and events, but there's something missing. They're all mixed together and on the stove—the only thing is that I don't have water, and a burnt soup isn't very delicious.

I personally start spending Mr. Badea's money, who guaranteed the discount of all my expenses. I quote, "If you need ten tanks, get twenty. Maybe some of them will break."

I start monitoring Bogdan, my main suspect. Nothing in his daily routine betrays his involvement, just as he knows exactly when and where I am. Or maybe he really is not involved, and all I'm doing is keeping my brain from finding solutions. What a shame that my nose can't sniff when the brain is altered. I make up my mind and from tomorrow on I'll start monitoring Alina more closely. I start with the beginning and give her a call.

"Good morning! Am I disturbing you?"

"Not at all. I was just having my coffee."

"Do you think we could have a coffee together? Off the record this time."

"Of course. Give me half an hour to get prepared, and I'll see you at …"

"Arcade, I know."

"No, I want to stay away from business. Let's meet at the Floare de Colț[7] restaurant."

"Perfect. I heard they make your coffee so strong that you can't stick your teaspoon in it."

Like a true gentleman, I wait for her in front of the restaurant, to open the door for her. Just fine, we're among the few clients, and this offers some privacy. Sitting at the table, I break the silence.

"I heard you were away in Cyprus."

"Greece."

"Details—they're neighbors."

"But details make the difference."

"And how was your trip?"

"More work than pleasure; we had to hold lectures and conferences every day."

"About?"

---

7 Floare de Colț – Lion's foot, edelweiss

"Details. I don't think it's the time now to tell you about all that."

"But details make the difference."

"Well, mainly about—"

"Just joking, no need for details."

Of course I don't need details. Her hesitation to give me a straight answer was more than enough to find out what I wanted to know.

"Do you think Marius will return?"

"I don't know what to think. Things are very dubious and don't link up. Somewhere, something is missing."

"Yeah ..."

"After all, what about the training camp?"

"He wanted to get away from home, to distance himself from the stress there, from problems."

"He's still a kid. What problems could he have at this age and not be able to solve them? Let's get serious."

"The fact that he grew up mostly by himself required him to mature earlier."

"Casinos, clubs, debts. Good way to grow up."

"Maybe I was also wrong toward him."

A few moments of complete silence, I watch her as she mixes her coffee. It's as if she had sugar cane in her cup and it had to be crushed and processed in order to obtain sugar before it could be dissolved. I had created a true vortex in my cup, and with the tail of my eye I searched for any lost fly to transform into a castaway, but the restaurant is a luxury one—no insect wing in sight. I think they hired chameleons to stalk and catch any living creature.

"How about going to my place?" She says in a nonchalant fashion.

Superb, I'll have the chance to search around her house legitimately. Looks like the night in Arcade when I took her to her home hurt her ego and she wants a revenge. Too bad she won't get the chance.

"Sounds good. Do you have any refreshments at home?"

"I probably do."

We stand and immediately the waiter shows up. He's either a medium or he has been standing the whole time next to us, simulating a piece of furniture. I pay, and we leave by her car to her house. A very orderly girl, nothing dubious in the car, everything in its place—the review mirror on the windshield, the gearshift between seats, the wheel in front of the driver, and a cup holder.

Well, well! Could her house also be so tidy? I'm sure I'll find a big nothing, but it's worth trying. Tock … and tock, and here comes tick, and this is how time goes fast. We get to her home. I let her go in first, in case there's a house dog resembling that on the gate sign warning, "Attention, bad dog! Come in at your own risk." I follow her and scan the area: no sign of a dog, not even a small dog house or a cluster of feces on the perfectly uniform lawn.

"Where's the dog from the photo on the gate?"

"There is none. The photo is just part of my system to scare off thieves."

"And the other part?"

"The alarm system never fails."

We go in. I feel like an astronaut going for a walk out on the ship and getting lost in the universe. A lot of space, few decorations or furniture. A few paintings, in red and green. I stand in front of one and pretend to be profoundly impressed.

Could this be made by the same painter who uses only green and red in painting a landscape, not to transpose the infinite nature of the universe and to eulogize the trauma though which our planet goes through, and the fact radiation is jeopardizing our health. Or maybe it's a simple coincidence?

"Nice way of painting a landscape, only using red and green!"

"I didn't know you knew anything about art. I like it too. It's a gift from my cousin."

I bet it's a gift from her, and I bet her name is Ingrid; otherwise, I would have known nothing about art.

I was admiring the pictures on her walls which for me were resembling human vomit after eating spinach with tomato sauce, but in fact I was looking for something through the house, something useful … something. Stop pushing! I don't know what! Something. And I found something, not because it helped me with my investigation, but to lift my spirit. She was coming with two glasses of something. No, not the something I was looking for. A random something. Small talk kept us company while the drink was running down our throats. The atmosphere was heating up around us, and already the situation seemed to be getting out of control. Hormones are going wild, and she seems to understand that, because the buttons of her blouse were allowing the bra to present its contents, just like a chef who's presenting you some kind of food on a tray, with a name so complicated that it gets you full even before you start eating it.

"It's getting rather late."

"Late for what?"

"For anything. I could very well look an excuse you would believe and then leave, or I could just simply say that I have to leave. It's your choice."

I would have love to run around the house with her, especially since she has a body that would straighten the devil's horns, but my intuition tells me to stop. Since so far it hasn't failed me, I obey it, provided that if it's wrong, I'll put it for sale on the Internet.

I read disappointment on Alina's face. She tries to convince me to stay for a little while, but seeing that she doesn't stand a chance, she says, "Wait, I'll go too. I have to do some shopping."

She takes out the wallet from her purse and counts the cash. I get to make a short inventory—a few cards, identification cards, several folded pieces of paper, and some business cards. Nothing out of the ordinary.

We leave, and in the car I press a couple of keys on my phone without her noticing, and suddenly the phone starts ringing. I pick it up and answer.

"Dan here, who's there?"

"…"

"When? Now? Okay, I'll get there in the morning! I'll call you when I arrive!"

I hang up and turn to her.

"It's an emergency. I have to get to Bucharest as soon as possible. Can you drop me off at the train station?"

"Yes, it's on our way, anyway. What happened?"

"Nothing out of the ordinary. I left the hot water running and it killed the flowers hanging on the balcony."

"You have a really well-developed sense of humor."

"It's directly proportional to my brain." Two for the cop, zero for the arrogant girl who thinks *I'm the goddess of Earth and no one can get to me unless I allow it!*

I find a train that leaves in twenty minutes, meaning I'll get to the capital sometime in the middle of the night. I also call Cezar.

"Hi, kid, how's it hanging?"

"Hi, boss, I was just looking for you."

"Quit looking for me. I found myself. I'm leaving to Bucharest, and

I'll be back as soon as possible. If I'm right I'll be back even tomorrow. You can sleep in my room while I'm gone!"

"Is it serious, boss?"

"Pretty serious, someone stole the light bulb on the stair and now it's pitch dark. It's not serious, but it's linked to the investigation. I'm on a new and clean track. If you have nothing to do, hang on to Bogdan. Maybe you'll manage to find out something."

With one finger I hang up and with the other I call the future host for my cocoon.

"Hi, Ingrid, how are you?"

"Dan, What a nice surprise! Nothing new. I'm at my workshop, painting and getting bored."

"Will I disturb if I come and shatter your boredom?"

"Of course not! But where are you now?"

"On my way to you. I'll be there in a few hours."

"Great, I can't wait to see you."

"Please make me a huge coffee if you want a dialogue and not a monologue on your side."

At the train station, I immediately disappear in a taxi and give the driver the address of the workshop. The artist probably has fetishes along with brushes and lots of paint. I arrive at the address. I think the taxi driver fooled me! I'm in front of a huge warehouse that looks extraordinarily deserted. What I'm doing there I really don't know, so I get the phone and call Ingrid. I can hear the phone ringing from inside the warehouse. I hang up and I start knocking on the door. I was about to find out that that wasn't a door, but a piece of corrugated sheet metal, because Ingrid opens a small door cut somewhere to my right, about the height of a cat standing on a cheetah. What do you want me to do? It's pitch black! She smiles and invites me inside. Inside is a complete contrast to the exterior. Here, the corrugated sheet metal is white and clean, and a few easels are scattered as if she painted on each one depending on the sun's position in the sky. There are many colors on the floor, actually lots of them, green and red. Brushes everywhere and she is full of paint, from ankles to her nose. Now I have two options, pretend and wallow with her until dawn, or take out my identification card and bombard her with a string of questions about her cousin.

My curiosity over a boy I haven't got the chance to meet wins the battle with my hormones. I take out my identification card, a useless formality, since she knows who I am, and I hand her the cuffs.

"I'm sorry to tell you, but you're under arrest!"

"Why such a hurry? We also have time to play. "She slowly approaches me, takes the handcuffs, and throws them loudly against the wall. The straps of her dress fall off her shoulders and she's left in only a pair of red boxers. I embrace her and start kissing her on the neck while my right hand plays with her hair. She smells like magnolias. She's pure, soft, and real. Time freezes, light slows down, colors run around us, the moon bedevils us, and yes, for a moment I leave everything aside. Soon I realize that the world is too tight for us both to fit in it, so we melt into one being. Her screams echo in the entire warehouse, and the easels shake in fear that we might tear them. When everything has calmed down and we have managed to catch our breath, I lift the handcuffs and approach her.

"Unfortunately, I'm not playing games." I take out of my pocket the photo received from the kidnappers. Initially, I thought those gray stripes in the background were because of the printer, which was probably dripping black ink, but they were actually shadows from the sheet metal's curves. And the newspaper he was holding was indeed *Gândul*, but not the edition from Craiova but rather the one from the capital. Coincidence or not? I'm about to find out.

I pull out two chairs facing each other and I ask her to take a seat.

"Do you know Alina Gruia?"

"Yes, we're cousins."

"Do you talk to each other often?"

"Whenever we have the opportunity."

"How about visits?"

"I haven't seen her in some time. Maybe a month or so."

"Was she alone the last time you saw her?"

"No, she came with a friend. Marius, a boy who of around seventeen."

"Did they come, or did she bring him?"

"How come? I don't understand."

"I mean, did he come willingly?"

"Yes, there were four other people with them. She said they were his bodyguards, because he's the son of a big businessman."

"Do you know the reason for their visit? Or was it just a courtesy visit?"

"They said they were passing through and that he wanted to see the workshop. I was busy, so she came alone with him, and then we all went out."

Incredible. I had a suspect … but a suspect for … for what? My only witness is telling me they came together and that he wasn't brought here by force.

"I trust you won't tell anything to Alina about my visit here."

"Why wouldn't I tell her?"

"Because you could endanger the life of a man who I don't even know … if he is still alive!"

"I don't think Alina could be involved in something like this."

"It doesn't matter—there still is the possibility that she is, and then things could get ugly."

"Whatever you say. You're the detective here."

"And you're the scourge of colorblind people. If you say one word I'll come here and force you to paint with blue!"

"Ha ha, just you dare!"

"I'm leaving. I'll see you when I finish my work there. I suggest you bring a fridge here, because when I'll come back we won't leave the workshop until you teach me to paint like Van Gogh."

"Only if you promise me that we'll walk again among the clouds."

"Clouds? I'll bring reflective vests so we don't bump into satellites."

Our discussion finishes with my last shirt button, and then I head back to the train station to get on the next train to Craiova. At least I found out that Alina is also involved. Now I just need to apply some pressure on her. If necessary, I'll start digging a grave, throw her there, and make her tell me everything she knows while I'm shoveling ground on top of her. But I have no free graveyard, nor a shovel, and I'm not even in the mood to start digging, but a serial killer did this in a movie and I think it's a very ingenious way of getting answers.

From the train I call and ask that Ingrid's phone be monitored. I don't believe she won't try to contact Alina and tell her what happened, so I give clear instructions: "If she says my name or Alina's on the phone, cut the relay!"

I also call Cezar to wait for me at the train station in the morning, holding a coffee so I can recognize him.

I have made huge progress in the investigation, but it's only hypothetical progress. Without the boy, either dead or alive, I have only the presumption of homicide. All I found out must stay between me and myself; not even Cezar will know, at least for now, because there is the risk that everyone will find out. It would be easier to publish the report in a newspaper.

Chapter VI

Or chapter "v" and "I" start growing next to it

I spend the next day at the hotel, browsing the TV channels and ordering coffee after coffee. Tragedy after tragedy on TV. I sit and wonder how is the population growing if so many people die every day.

"Look, Cezar, a landslide buried an entire village. Could it be that hard to see a mountain coming toward you?" Ding! And it's not the door. It's my head.

"Cezar, tomorrow morning we have to go somewhere. Until then, find out for me where Alina's parents are, I want to go and ask for their daughter's hand!"

The following morning finds us packing several cups of coffee for the road. We have to drive for about a hundred kilometers to Mr. Gruia's home village.

"Boss, but her parents are dead. How could you ask them for their daughter's hand?"

"I knew that, kid. It was only a metaphor. I actually want both her hands."

It's long and toilsome road. Wherever you look there are only corn and wheat fields. Croaking starlings are lining the sky, and the sun reflects in the asphalt, creating *fata morgana*.

We enter the main street in the village, the only one asphalted. On the left and right, there are some barefooted children playing. This lack of technology totally relaxes me, and I drive the car slowly so I can enjoy the silence and the hot, dusty air. We stop next to a few elders gathered to gossip on a bench.

"Good day. Do you happen to know where Mr. Gruia lived?"

Indications flow from all. I try to focus on only one while he's explaining where Mr. Gruia's house is. "God rest his soul. He was a hard-working man," they all reply.

The house is an old one, made of lattices walled with cow manure and yellow clay. An old technique, but very often used in the old villages of the country, where people didn't have cement and other construction materials. Later on, when these became accessible, they were too old to start demolishing and renovating. And the young ones don't stay in villages, leaving for the big cities in search of good jobs. Too bad—we have resources but don't know how to take advantage of them. I inspect the house from over the fence. It looks very shabby, which is explicable, since no one has lived here in four years.

I jump over the fence in two moves and open the gate for Cezar. We go inside the house and everything seems dead: dust, insects, flees, flies. We keep searching, and I find one of the rooms, which had two metal rings above the doorknob, probably in order to be locked with a bolt. I open it and go inside. A disordered bed, a chair, some leftover food on a table, and some papers in an envelope. My first thought was that Marius was kept here. I call Cezar over. He's out of my visual and auditory range; he definitely saw a fruit tree and is now feasting. I open the envelope and get to see they are tickets for Paris. I try to get them out of the envelope to see any more details, but to my surprise, nothing. Pitch black.

I don't know how long it's been, but I see light. Headache. Cezar! Cezar tied up, and so am I. I look for the envelope, which of course no longer exist. This really is an embarrassing situation. The room I studied earlier has now become our cell. Outside we can hear voices and fuss. Considering the sound of steps, there are four persons. Or only two, dancing a polka, which is highly unlikely. They have also taken my handcuffs and gun, but they didn't even use them on us. We're tied with thick ropes.

"Cezar, are you all right?"

"My arm hurts. I saw them coming and went toward them with my identification card. They grabbed my hand and someone hit me and I fell."

"Good. At least we're still alive. Did you manage to see their faces?"

"Just one. His head was shaved and had a tough look."

"Like all of Mihai's gorillas."

"Do you think he did this?"

"No way, but someone with access to his resources has likely recruited some of the men for personal use. This thought has been haunting me for some time now."

I begin to distinguish some of the voices outside. Either my head was hit too hard or one of them is speaking with a French accent—and very ungrammatical. I can hear cars leaving, among which is ours, which I recognize due to the sound of its engine.

"Cezar, so you still have the car keys?"

"No."

"Good, then you'll explain to the rental agency why we lost the car!"

I look around us in search of a way out. A double window is letting in light and has a grill between the two sheets of glass.

"Cezar, come next to me. Sit with your back toward me and lean over!"

Even if my request intrigued him a bit, he gets into position obediently. I turn my back to him and let him know that this will hurt. I lean over my back on his back and hit the window with my feet, which shatters. Of course, because of that move, we're both lying on the floor, with Cezar screaming in pain. I believe him, since a little earlier he complained about arm pains and now I've crushed them between ourselves. But our escape requires sacrifices. With a shard in my hand I start cutting the ropes. Hard job—they were of very good quality—but I managed. He repeats the process and sets me free. I pull the bed in front of the window, and I start relieving myself on the frame, but unfortunately my physiological reserves are finished, so it's Cezar's turn. The window had a grill, and even if it was strongly anchored on the frame, I cannot say the same about the house. With a bit of trust in our urinary skills, we manage to moisten the wall around the window, as this is only manure with yellow clay and twigs. Now, armed with chair legs, we scratch again and again through the wall. After a while, the frame weakens like the teeth of a preschooler; all we needed to get it out of the rudimentary "masonry" were some strong hits in its corners.

The moral: if you take someone prisoner, make sure they have a toilet in their room so they won't urinate on walls!

We get out on the street and go down the road we came, knowing it leads to the main street.

"Let's go, Cezar. Maybe we can find a bar!"

"Boss, I'm hungry, I'm sick, and you're in the mood for drinking?"

"The intense activity of today has dehydrated me, and plus, we need to find out who those guys are. And since news are always in bars, it's the perfect place!"

We go in a pub smelling like double-refined alcohol diluted with water and caramel and sold as cognac to the local people and above all of this, add the smell of sweat mixed with dust. This reminds me that I should not drink tap beer. Instead, I ask for four beers on the first order, one for Cezar and three for myself. People are staring strangely at us, a good sign—this means they all know each other and the outsiders don't get by unobserved. It's possible that we interrupted a meeting in plenum. And they keep on staring. I thought I could humor them. Knowing that all people in villages have a highly developed civic spirit and boundless respect toward men of the law, I pull out my ID, which, luckily, was still in my possession.

"Chief Quaestor Criminalistics, Dan Demetriad. We apologize that we didn't introduce ourselves in the first place, but we didn't want to disturb you."

"No problem, Mr. Chief. It's a good thing that you told us who you are. Otherwise ..."

"Otherwise?"

"How can we put this? There have been some outsiders around here, and they were in the mood for scandal."

"So you chased them out. Good move. Did you know anyone of them?"

"No, Officer, but we know where they're staying."

"Yes, yes! Another one intervened. I saw them in Mr. Gruia's yard. They stayed there for a few days. What they were up to, I don't know."

"Did they come alone?"

"No, sir. They were with that daughter of his, Ileana."

"Alina?"

"Yea, Alina, and a cousin of hers. I think it is Traian's son."

"He wasn't, Nelu. Traian has a daughter. She lives in Bucharest."

"And what did those guys look like?"

"They were sort of nervous, always baleful, just one of them was more thinnish, but I don't think he was one of us. He spoke in a different language. A neighbor told us that she saw them there today, and they heard him yelling through the yard, "*Mere, mere.*"[8]

"He was singing to them, Nelu, so that they'd grow big."

They all startlaughing, which brought with it, the relief of finding out who we are and that we are not part of the "bad guys." Moreover, they're very attentive with us, making sure we don't lack anything or that there isn't too much smoke in the pub, in which case they'd open a window.

Seems like I manage to find out more than I expected. We spend all night in the pub, and at the first rays of sun we're sitting nicely in the train station. I'm leaning against a tree and Cezar is vomiting next to a wall. We manage to get to the city before noon, and go straight to the hotel where we order chops and pickled cucumbers for breakfast to calm our nausea, then sleep. We have time for all the other things, but tomorrow.

The first trip we made in the morning was to the police station. Here, the same inspector offers to help me. I was hoping he forgot, but ...

"Greetings, Mr. Demetriad. I wanted to ask you, that night when there was a scandal in Club Cleopatra, my men told me that you took the victim to the hospital. How is he doing?"

"He's fine. I threw him in the Jiu River, because he was covered in blood, and I didn't manage to pull him back to the surface. But don't worry, I tied a piece of concrete to his foot to make sure the water won't take him away."

His eyes popped out of his head like those of a snail. He didn't know whether he should laugh or be frightened by my story. He seemed more comfortable laughing, so I had to listen for a couple of minutes to his gruntings, meantime frantically looking for the location where Alina had spent her two years in France. I find the name of a little village near Dijon.

"Good sauce. Is it just a coincidence, or this is where it comes from?"

"What?" replies the inspector, flooded with tears of laughter.

---

8 "Apples, apples."

"Nothing. Do you have access to banking transactions from here?"

"No, you can go to the headquarters of the bank and they'll definitely help you."

Perhaps you're wondering why Alina is in the police database.? Well, just about anyone in contact with Mihai has a record, and most of them are under surveillance, which initially made me think that none of them are involved in the disappearance, because the police would have intervened immediately. However, considering the clues I have so far, it looks like Bogdan and also Alina are involved. I repeat, hypothetically. I only have a dead dog, a skilled (or idiotic) veterinarian (I haven't really decided about him), and a girl who lies about the last moment when she saw the boy but who, according to a witness, was with him. So far, no sign of violence or kidnapping.

I'm leaving the station, heading for Mihai. It seems the shock produced by the kidnapping and the failed attempt to get the boy back home was short lived. Things are back into normal in their family, as if he boy had left for a vacation in Ibiza.

"Any sign so far?" I ask instead of greeting.

"No, nothing. All we can do is wait."

"Maybe you. I'm not losing any minute more. Yesterday I went to visit the house of Alina's parents."

"And did you find anything?"

"Almost."

"What do you mean, almost?"

"I mean, there we found some plane tickets left on a table, probably forgot by mistake, but before I could look at them in detail, I got smacked on the back of my head and we woke up tied."

"And how did you manage to get out of there? Who did this?"

"We don't know yet, but you could give me the sheets with the schedule of your security employees for the last month. I'm sure some of them are involved."

"My men? Never! They're loyal to me. They have been working for me for a long time."

"I believe you, but life's an auction. Whomever offers more wins."

I cash in a nice amount of money from him, for travel and expenses, and I train Cezar about what he has to do while I'm gone. In case I don't report daily by phone, he should send a team to look for me. The first plane to France is mine. I also want to try my luck with Alina's host.

I'm thinking that this might be their next move, considering the tickets I found inside the house. During the several flight hours, I go through those schedules. None of them seemed to have the time to assist with the kidnapping. Those who were off duty on the day of the kidnapping were working during other key moments in the succession of events, so either the security employees were all involved in a global plot though which them, along with the strongest countries of the world were conceiving an evil plan to get Marius out of business, either they really weren't involved.

I arrive in Paris. People here give me a strange feeling. They seem, as one of them has said, "a nation of bourgeois who do not admit this fact, attacking the other because they are." It is very crowded, and it seems as if everyone knows exactly what they have to do and where they must get. So do I. I head to my final destination, a village located at a little over fifty kilometers away from Paris. I quickly find a bus that will take me there. My French is sufficient to speak with the locals and I manage to find out that Selene hosted a girl who came from Romania a while ago, and someone offers to take me there.

The difference between rural areas in Romania and rural areas in France is not big, is colossal. Here, I find a one-story villa and so much glass that you could see what's happening in the back of the house just by looking at it. A girl opens the door and I soon realize that she's Selene, the one was looking for. She is tall and slender, elegantly dressed and with a warm look. Red curls fall down her shoulders in waves, and her lips move strangely, in French.

"Good day. May I help you?"

"Good day. Dan is my name. I think you can. I wouldn't have travelled more than two thousand miles just to drink water."

Her face contorts in a grimace. It seems I didn't manage to get to her heart, which is one of the places I'm not quite interested to be right now, since my idea of finding an abandoned house where I could find a boy was shattered. Internationally I am a nobody, and my ID is a simple plastified piece of paper, but I could contact the police here to assist me, a fact which she seemed aware of, since she offered her cooperation without asking too many questions. She invites me in for a cup of coffee, and since time is precious, I get right to the subject.

"Do you speak to Alina often?"

"Honestly, no. After she left we never spoke. While she stayed here, our relationship was that of host-guest. We never became friends."

"This is pretty obvious. One will never be able to put two silver foxes in the same cage."

She smiles and thanks me for the compliment. I'm glad I didn't express exactly what I was thinking. Such a house, with such endowments, requires a large amount of money, and she's been "working" for several years as unemployed. Her husband is mostly away to Paris, without having a regular workplace so I really wonder how do they get the money. After about half an hour of talking I decided to put her on the suspect list, because she's avoiding giving me concrete answers. Maybe she was doing that only because she was scared that she'd be arrested for the other dirty laundry she has.

"Did she have any friends here? Did she hang out in clubs, bars?"

"Yes, she'd leave just about every night, but I didn't know who she was going out with, and I didn't care as long as she didn't get into trouble. Just one person brought her here several times. There was a guy who was picking her up and dropping her off by car."

"Do you remember his name?"

"Maurice was how he introduced himself, but I know nothing more about him."

Interesting and useful, but only half of it. Now I have to search for a Maurice in a France. It seems that I'm going from the beach to the desert, and from the sea to the ocean. I don't know exactly what I wanted to find out from her, so I left, disappointed by the meeting. I started thinking, an activity which, for the moment, doesn't bring much satisfaction to me.

Chapter VII

Or the previous chapter
with another "I"

"Cezar, how are things going?"

"Slowly, boss. I haven't managed to find anything new."

"I had a partial success here. I need you to do to the bank and verify some transactions for me."

"Did you find any solution, boss?"

"Solution? Yes, a solution for gluing my boots, so that I don't worry about tearing them apart on your ass when I'll receive the telephone invoice home. Jokes aside, learn from me, Cezar, that there are no solutions, but only active forces. They must be created, and only then solutions emerge. Now get to work. Stop wasting time."

"Ready, boss. I'm leaving now and I'll call you when I get there."

Tick tock tick tock ding, and I answer.

"Look for the last transactions made by Alina. Actually no, search starting with the date of Marius' disappearance."

"Shopping, a cash withdrawal, bills payments, nothing out of the ordinary."

"Okay, check the other banks where she has accounts and call me."

And again tic-tacs from Mr. Time and a coffee savored at a lounge on the Champs-Élysées. I checked into a hotel in Paris, because here I have the best chance to find out anything, and above this I had easy access to any part of the country.

"Boss, the same small transactions everywhere, just a large amount of money withdrawn a week after the disappearance."

"Clever girl. Cash is more difficult to monitor, if not impossible. Good, Cezar. If I need anything else I'll contact you."

I hang up and I start studying the people passing by the lounge. I do so absently, because there was an immense battle going on inside my mind. I felt like a two-year-old child who has some geometrical pieces and continues to push a cube into a hole reserved for a prism.

Interesting. If you watch the people more closely, you can observe relaxation, stress, thoughts, problems. Their facial tics give them away, their inclined head, straight back and rigid walk. Some slowly throw their feet, while others step heavy and rush. Some laugh, others hug. People tend to hide when they're under the impression that they have done something wrong or that they are being watched. I also throw myself in a world of meaningless thoughts, and my eyes rest in my cup of coffee which, now comes very fast toward me, spilled by a clumsy and rushed guy. I raise my eyes to see the one who did it, the one who is guilty for making contact with my table, sending this vital fluid to waste.

"*Merde!*" he says, upset at the limb, and after he looks at me kindly and politely apologizes. I look at him and smile. This little man has no clue that he offered me an important piece to my puzzle. Yes! This is it! *Mere!*[9] The apples the foreigner was screaming for in the yard were nothing other than curses. Curses in French! Maurice was at just a few meters away from me. Maybe he is even the one who gave me the blow that sent me to the world of darkness. I feel like a prophet, only my sublime prophecies refer to the past. If I'd had a crystal globe, I'd manage to see in the future and to find him. Maybe by now he is already someone else. Maybe he assumed an Arab name and is now called Milkah al Cheesed and is the sheik of Yoghurtania. Returning to my interlocutor, he offers to buy another coffee for me.

"Only if you don't spill this one too," I reply.

"Again, I apologize. I was in a hurry and by mistake I hit your table with my foot."

"I know that. I was here when it happened. Please learn that I'm not going to accept your apologies."

"Why?" he asks, stunned. "I even offered to replace your coffee,

---

9   Apples.

and you accepted. I considered to be a confirmation of the fact that you accept my apologies."

"I accepted because we're responsible for our actions. I think it's only natural."

"But I don't understand. Why you won't accept my apologies?"

"Does it matter? You won't remember me anyway, and this episode will pass unnoticed."

"Yes, but—"

"Have a seat, please. Have you ever assisted in a trial where the defendant recognizes his guilt and regrets it?"

"No," he answers, while his eyes clearly point out for me that he has difficulties finding the meaning in this discussion.

"The only difference is that this shortens the duration of the trial. This doesn't change the deed in any way. A murder is still a murder."

"I find your comparison a bit exaggerated. Still, this is only a small inattention."

"Pay attention to the inattention! A little vigilance never does any harm. Out of principle I don't accept apologies, because, in turn, I don't apologize and I take responsibility for my actions. At best I might say that if I could turn back time, I'd do things differently. But since time doesn't belong to us, I am, let's say, a bit outdated."

This makes him think for a minute. Maybe in the future he will be more attentive in cases when the end really does matter. He gets up, baffled, and signals the waitress that he wants to pay. He takes his card out of the wallet, pays, and then reaches out to me, smiling.

"If I could turn back time, I'd pay more attention not to hit any table."

"Thank you for the coffee! I hope you know that there's something very special in it!"

"Coffee, milk, sugar, and water." He smiles happily.

"And a lot of truth!"

He turns around and leaves twice as baffled, scratching the back of his head. Following him with my eyes, with my ear in my phone and my mouth full of words, I wait for my good Cezar to answer.

"Where are you, young man?"

"On my way to the hotel, boss, why?"

"I need you to go to the bank and verify some transactions for me."

I think I have a déjà-vu.

"All due respect, boss, what did you consume?"

"Nothing for now, but I fell how you slowly consume my patience."

"I went to the banks just earlier."

"And you blew them up when you left, so you can't go there again? Cezar, the mistake is mine. You didn't check the right person! Look for the international transactions made to France from the card of Ingrid Gruia. I'm sure there will be some, and they will take me where I need to go! And so that you see that I care, search at only one of the banks. My gut tells me that there you'll find what we're interested in.

The same gut transmits through my stomach that we're vertiginously approaching a calamity: starvation. During the time I'm spending shoving several comestible items down my throat, the kid confirms the presence of several transfers made a week after the boy went missing, to an account opened in France.

"Now verify the number of the account where the money went, and we'll know how we can trace Maurice."

"You're right, boss. The account belongs to a Maurice Villain. How did you know that?"

"The crystal globe spoke, Cezar!"

"Are you into witchcraft, boss?"

"No, Cezar, no. It was a metaphor."

"Ummmm, yes. It seems that we constantly withdrew money from an ATM in Lyon. That's probably where he lives."

"Olé! Give me the address. It's perfect!"

I'll spare you the boredom of the road, which personally doesn't bother me. I always enjoyed travelling, seeing new places, new people. It helps me relax. Ever since I was a child I went with my father on different missions, of course the harmless ones. I wanted to become a policeman like him, to have a belly, money, and respect from people, but only now I learn how much he worked to have all this. I try to remember the last vacation I benefited from, but it's impossible. Since I finished the Academy, I managed only for one week to stay away from murders, kidnappings, and chaos. I think I'll decree one week without violence, so we can all relax. Not that I'm complaining.. My work schedule is pretty relaxed, and if there weren't situations where I was being beaten, held at gunpoint, tied, or deprived of sleep, it would really be perfect.

It's relatively difficult to find the address—after all, I'm new in town—but I find the ATM. I stand in front of it and look around. A cemented park full of people, several shops, and a long street full of houses. The registered address of Maurice is in Bordeaux, and I don't think I'd be successful if I went there and knocked on the door. It's more exciting to start as far from the obvious as possible when it comes to criminals. I slowly advance down the street. I'm looking for a house that doesn't look like it's inhabited by a family with children, or that's very well taken care of—it doesn't seem his style. There are only two like this. I decide not to make a big fuss about my arrival, so I jump over the fence into the yard of the first house and walk around it. I force the back door and manage to get inside. Luckily no one is here. Rummaging through the kitchen, I find some ready-to-eat food in the fridge. It seems that those who live here don't have much time to cook. They're frozen, so they don't tell me much about the last time the refrigerator was filled, so I move on.

There's some dirty flatware and dishes in the sink. I pick up a plate smelling like sea food. The sour cream sauce is hardened; it's more than two days old. I find some books and papers thrown on the table in the living room, among them a Romanian–French dictionary. It's either a coincidence, or I arrived exactly where I needed. In the attic I find some clothes thrown on the bed. The chaos here shows that someone left in a hurry or that there was an altercation between several persons. A few artificial flowers are thrown on the floor. I think they rather flew off the vase, so I lie on the floor on my belly to inspect it better. It smells like flooring detergent and chlorine, a lot of chlorine whipped in a hurry, because I can see white dry marks on the surface of the parquet. I get a knife from the kitchen and stick it between two pieces of parquet, exactly where they're joined. I manage to separate them and lift them up. I can see the spots left by bleach and a few red spots. Exactly as you suspected. These are marks made by spaghetti Bolognese sauce. Excuse me, we're in France—it clearly is strawberry jam from croissants. I take a closer look and conclude these are traces of blood. Most likely the victim was hit with the vase, then collapsed on the floor and bled before waking up or being carried away. I decide to stay here as long as I need to and I settle down as if it were my home, especially since I discovered the wonder making machinery of the XXIst century: the espressor!

The food from the fridge and pizza keeps me alive for almost a week here. The abundance of coffee and French wine staved off dehydration, and this is how I survived better than a Bedouin who got lost in the desert without food or water. I am a true survivor! One evening, my waiting ends, because I can hear a key turning in the door.

I get up from the couch so that the surprise is a great one. It rarely happens that my blood pressure rises during these moments, but I didn't know who is on the other side of the door, and this makes me uneasy. What if it isn't Maurice, and it is just a simple French guy, bored with his life, returning from a vacation after beating his wife in the room upstairs, exasperated by life and nervous because, after that, she moved back with her mother? These trips in search of the kidnappers brought me clues each time, but not a docile person telling me to my face, "Congratulations, you won!" But I know that only happens at Monopoly, so I maintain my vigilance and I choose not to throw the dice. The door opens toward me and the individual reaches out to turn on the light, a gesture that makes my job easier, because he immediately sees me standing and holding my gun, just two meters away from him. Total silence. Is this thanks to my personal charm, or does this beauty made by Smith & Wesson inspire more respect? Honestly, I don't care if Smith or Wesson are more pleasant than me. At least I'm alive. I study him and realize I could miss if I shot toward him from this distance, because he's slightly fatter than a pen. His cadaverous face, hollow cheeks, and acne clearly indicate that his childhood wasn't very nice and that all the girls avoided him because of his immense pimples. He had an empty and tired look, definitely coming from a long distance. I greet him politely and ask him to identify himself.

"Maurice Villain."

I'm so lucky!

"Welcome!"

"Who are you?"

"Excuse my impoliteness. I'm tired. Dan is my name."

"And what are you doing in my house?"

"Considering the amount of time I spent here, I might well ask you the same question. Have a seat. Would you like a coffee? I think you might be tired after such a long road." I signal him with my gun to sit down on the couch. I sit in front of him, in the armchair, at a distance that's sufficient to shoot him in case he tries anything. The table between us offers me support in case he makes a run at me.

"Look, I have a gun and you don't. This offers me an advantage against you. Don't try to be a hero, because you're not the first person I would shoot, not deadly, but enough to calm you down and get some answers from you. If you want to cooperate, this is to your own advantage; otherwise, I will be obliged to use violence. So let's begin. Where have you been gone all this time?"

I only manage to get an idiot look from him. And he keeps looking, searching for excuses, plans and ideas in his head.

"What are you doing now, reading my subtitle?" I interrupt his moment of melancholia.

"I don't see why I would talk to a stranger who broke into my house and now threatens me with a gun."

"And besides that, the jerk emptied your fridge, also!"

"I'm glad you find this situation amusing. I can see nothing funny about it and I am asking you very politely to leave before you get into trouble."

"*Mon cher,* be careful not to lose yourself among words and to be sent to hell. The only exorcist I know has left for a crusade. My advice is to communicate before you make me lose my patience!"

"I went to visit my relatives to Nice. Happy?"

"No, that's not okay. We try again. Where were you?"

"I already told you. To visit my parents in Nice."

"Is it just me, or do you think I'm stupid? Here, take these, I'm sure you'll manage to put them on yourself." And I give him the handcuffs over the table.

"Am I arrested? What for?"

"Did anybody say I'm a cop? I'm a criminal who bought the cuffs for two euros from a hunting store, and I want to try them before I go in the woods with them to tie up bears. I wouldn't want to tie a killing machine with sewing thread. So stop asking so many questions and put the handcuffs on."

"Until I see an ID and an arrest warrant, I am doing nothing. I have no idea who you are and what you're doing in my house, so get lost!"

This boy wants to play and he does it on my nerves. I hit the table with my foot, and it slides toward him and hits his locomotor apparatus straight in the tibias. I think I was too brutal, considering the sound of the impact and grimace on his face. I immediately get up from the armchair and go to him. He didn't have time to react; the pain was too big for him to think anything of me. Two more moves and there he stands, handcuffed and facing down on the table, like a calf at rodeo.

"Good. Now let's resume. Where were you gone?"

"In Nice! He shouts in despair."

Bang. His head hits the table with a blank sound.

"Each time you lie, the table will hit you in the head. This will happen until you either pass out or decide to tell the truth. To come to your aid, your parents live in Bordeaux. I know enough about you to know when you're lying."

"I was gone to visit someone I know in Romania."

"Whose name is?"

"Alina. Gruia Alina."

"There, see how it's healthier to discuss things like buddies? Have you been to Romania before, or was this your first time?"

"First time!"

Bang. The same noise from his head hitting the table. I made sure that his eyes were perpendicular to the table, so these short blows would crush his nose, a terrible pain, difficult to bear.

"*Pfff,* and I had just started to trust you!"

"I was there before, a month or a month and a half ago, something like that."

"No problem, we'll find the exact date right away. Get up!"

I throw him on the armchair and, watching him, I go grab the bag he left at the entrance. I search and find his passport. Visas … visas, and more visas. Look, you were in Romania in June also and stayed for two weeks. Where exactly?"

"At her place, a house somewhere in the rural area."

Looks like I'm right again. He's the one screaming for "*mere*" in the yard.

Now I must find out from him as much as I can about the boy, and I'm sure he won't admit everything from the beginning, so I put his feet on the table, take his shoes off, and with the shoelaces I tie his feet to those of the table so that he is lying to go for you and half on the table and half on the armchair. Very uncomfortable and very hard to get out of that position. I go to the kitchen and get the bowl full of hot coffee from the espressor, and a cup. I return to the table and pour some magic liquor in the cup, preparing my soul for a boring interrogation.

"What did you do with the boy?"

"What boy? "

I get the coffee bowl and pour it on his foot. I didn't know an espressor keeps coffee so hot! His skin immediately turns red and, to make the scene truly grotesque, the poor guy starts moaning like a bull who has just gotten his share of unwanted sex from another bull.

"Quiet down, you'll wake the neighbors. Stop lying. If we'll keep going like this, I'll finish the coffee and start using something more painful, something what will do permanent damage. Do you know Marius Badea?"

"Yes!"

"When did you meet him?"

"When I was in Romania for the first time Then Alina came with him where I was staying."

"Were they together?"

"No, they came together. They don't make a couple."

"And what did you do next?"

"They said they wanted to go to France on vacation, but she was busy in Craiova, so only he went."

"Why did you return to Romania the second time?"

"Because Alina called me and said she couldn't talk over the phone about such a thing and that I must go there as soon as possible."

"This means your financial situation isn't that bad, right?"

"Actually, it is, but she paid for the road."

"And why did you return to the elders' house before leaving?"

"We hadn't left yet. Alina told us to stay there for a few days more, because she wants to get rid of an inconvenient cop first."

"Interesting. Did she say anything about how she was going to do that?"

"No, she only said that she'll take him to her house and then he would disappear for good."

"Why did you hit and tie the two men who were in Alina's house?"

"Because they were burglars, breaking into the house!"

"Right, and as punishment you stole their car and locked them tied up in the house. If I wasn't so amused by your answers, I would decorate your toes with barbed wire and I'd make you dance Step! What did you do with the car?"

"It's in the airport parking garage."

"And the key?"

"The key is hidden between the front bumper and license plate."

Great! Remind me to call Cezar and ask him to go get it. I got rid of an expense that would have made a serious hole in my budget.

"Returning to the first part, namely the second visit. All three of you returned to France? Where did you live?"

"Here."

"And where is he now?"

"He left."

"This is what I suspected, but where and whom with?"

"With the three bodyguards his father sent to accompany him."

Interesting, looks like the father's dirty. Could this be a setup planned by the entire family? This clearly results from the discussion.

"Where did he leave?"

"I don't know. He never called me. I was only in contact with Alina."

"Whose blood is that in the attic?"

This created a shock in his eyes. He probably didn't expect that anyone would find traces, and he was hoping that I bought the story with the boy leaving.

"It's mine. I had an open wound on my hand and I probably hit myself in my sleep and dripped a small amount of blood."

Again, the reason is stupid, but this time it makes me uneasy. I promise the man that if he lies again I'll do something even worse, but for now I have no idea, so I put my fist on his jaw, closely followed by moaning. I prepare for the second one from a long string of fists, sufficient for changing his menu from solid food to baby mash. He realizes on his own that I would stop only if a meteorite hit the house right then, so he decides to continue.

"It's … his. It was an accident. He tripped, he fell and hit his head."

"And where did you take him?"

"He left with Alina right after the accident."

"So he wasn't dead, passed out, dismantled, unboned or anything else that would prevent from functioning as a whole?"

"No, nothing serious."

"What did Alina want to tell you that you needed to travel there?"

"We didn't have the chance to talk because the cop had escaped, and we had problems with the two, so we had to leave."

"Good, you can calm down. The coffee got cold, anyway. I'm going to see the city's lights. Our lightning interrogation is over."

"Aren't you going to untie me?"

"Help yourself!" I throw him the keys for the cuffs toward the table. Unfortunately I missed, so it will take a while longer until he manages to escape.

"And after all, who are you?"

"You can call me Sophie. We'll not meet again soon, anyway. *Au revoir*, you contortionist!"

On the contrary, I couldn't wait to see him again. I knew that he will panic and call Alina to tell her, and their next move will be carefully monitored by me.

I leave and check into a hotel in Lyon. Cezar said that Alina left to another conference, also in Greece. So, like the last time, she will probably arrive here. I follow Maurice and, as expected, the next day he goes to the airport, where he meets with our dear medical student, who juices her brain at various medical conferences. Not. I see them talking. Then he takes a bag from the car's trunk and they go into the airport together. No sign of them for a few good hours. They definitely left by another plane. I grab my phone and call my loyal sidekick, Cezar.

"Cezar, do you have any news?"

"Regarding what, boss?"

"Regarding the escape of penguins from the zoo in Ghana."

"Well, Alina left again, as I told you. Bogdan hangs around clubs and veterinary clinics, and Marius hasn't shown up."

"And look how we wasted time to point out the obvious again! Contact Mihai to call Alina, and meanwhile, talk with our magician to trace the call."

"Got it, I'm on it!"

Maybe you're asking why I chose the harder way. First of all, I can't even realize why, and secondly, I don't want Alina to know that I am on to her. As expected, she didn't answer her phone. That doesn't bother me one bit, and while expecting for Cezar's phone call I check at the airport all planes that took off after Alina's arrival. There is a flight to Bordeaux, and under the influence of my ID the boys from the airport are nice enough to give me the passenger list, and the two are on it. So I reserve a ticket for the next day, with the same destination, then sank into a flavored coffee, which helps me to be awake in my sleep, to think efficiently. Night replaced the day, only to switch places again the next morning, which finds me in the airport, waiting to board. The flight itself lasts less than all formalities, and here I am in Bordeaux!

Chapter VIII

Or, simply, the chapter before last

Here, I feel like a flea sitting on the back of a Carpathian sheepdog's head. Crowded. Very crowded! Lots of tourists who came to enjoy very much sun. In short, everything here is "very." The Mediterranean air refreshes my brain. I feel the need to drop everything, to dress into some shorts with floral motifs, a pair of fancy sunglasses, and a fisherman's hat, then lie down on the sand. But I'll postpone my vacation for a little while in the hope that my plan will succeed. Not having any concrete starting point, I decide to visit Maurice's family. With a little help from my loyal recruit, I get the address. Since I don't want to raise suspicions, I don't go there directly, but I show up smiling at the door of the neighbors across the street, where an old man with few hairs and many years of activity in the world of the living answers the door.

"Good day! Dan is my name, police officer is my job. Can I come in?"

"Why? Did I do anything? I have no business with the police. Get away from here!"

"You did nothing—calm down—I need your help. May I come in?"

"No, what kind of police officer are you?"

"One whose cover will soon be blown if you won't let me in! Here's my passport, my driver's license—what other documents do you wish to see?"

"But what's your business with me?"

"Sir, it's very important that I come in. If I'm seen by Mr. Villain there is a great chance he'll run, and I'll also leave this sand trail they left, and everything goes to hell. What don't you understand?" Already I was feeling my head on fire. How much I would have loved in that moment to smack him over the face and leave him senseless. My shock was even greater when on his sunburned face a smile appeared, which soon turned into a sarcastic laughter, revealing his yellow teeth.

"Well, anyway, Mr. Villain can see you anytime."

"Of course. And the Tooth Fairy works in a brothel to increase her income. His contract on Earth was terminated?"

"He's up in heaven."

"When did this happen?"

"About a month ago."

"And his wife?"

"He was divorced. His son, Maurice, used to come by, but only rarely."

"I understand. Did he come for the funeral?"

"Yes, him and his wife."

"Wife?"

"Yes, a tall girl with long hair. She doesn't really look like she's around here. I'd say she's somewhere from the East. I also saw them yesterday around here."

"Could you please tell me where Mr. Villain is?"

"What good will that do? You'll not find out anything from him anyway."

"Usually a dead man says more than one alive. And dead bodies don't lie."

"Go to the end of the street, make a left, and you'll see the tower from the chapel. It's easy to get there."

Our relationship started so badly and finished so well. I apologize for the trouble and head for the cemetery. Pythagorean paradise, all arranged symmetrically and very well defined. I go in and arrive between hundreds of graves. If I had started to read each cross in search for the grave, I would have probably found my ending here, so I look around for a person who's still alive who might help me.

"Sir, sir!" I shout to a guy in his fifties walking around the graves.

"Hello. Is something wrong?" he answers, glad that he's not alone here.

"No, I mean not really. I understood that a friend of mine is checked in here, and I did not have the chance to present my condolences. Villain is his name. He left us about a month ago."

"Yes, yes, I remember. I used to know him."

"Could you take to him?"

"Yes, follow me. He was my friend. What's your name? Maybe he told me about you."

"I don't think you know me. Michel Dregtot is my name."[10]

I fixed it again, I always fix it all.

"No, unfortunately, he didn't tell me anything."

We get to the tomb and I start inspecting the place. I don't know what I'm looking for or even why I came to the cemetery, but a genius never makes mistakes, and if he happens to be wrong, he does do intentionally. I do the search with my hands joined and my head inclined as if for a prayer, because he also remained with me and I had to maintain appearances.

"I did not expect him to die. He was also cheerful and healthy. When I learned he suffered a heart attack out of the blue, it made my hair stand on end."

"It happens, in the end, we all go, sooner or later. Life is just a phase between birth and death." I finish my speech filled with spirituality for another short moment of silence, and then I come again.

"We hadn't seen each other in several years. He wrote that he had gained a lot of weight. Maybe this is why his heart weakened."

"That's a good one, Peter gained weight? He was even thinner than his son. He probably said that so that you won't be concerned about him."

"Clearly! Poor him. Thank you for your help. Stay healthy!" I tell him and turn around.

"Thank you. You too."

I head for the exit smiling. How strange those words sounded, "stay healthy," in a graveyard. It's a good thing the dead can't speak, or else they'd give me the edge of their tongues. At least Mr. Villain did, indirectly, it's true, but things are clear for me.

I look on the street so that I won't be seen, and I enter in the yard of the house in search of an opening through which to enter. I manage to push the airing window of the cellar and, holding my gun, I go scouting around the

---

10 "Dregtot"—coming from the construction in Romanian language "dreg tot," meaning "fix it all," thus, the name could be translated as "Michel Fix-it-all" (translator's note).

house. Total silence and no sign of the suspects. I find the bags I saw at the airport, but unopened. They probably didn't want to lose too much time around here. I go upstairs and search through the rooms. I find Marius' baggage in a lumber box. I open it and see that they're all crammed in a hurry, and this tells me that when they left from Lyon they did it hastily and didn't get the chance to arrange them. I go out in the backyard, where I see a space designed for filling free time. A coquet construction of brick covered the barbeque, under which there still was some ashes. I stick my gun in the residue and I find several pieces of clothing that I don't get to touch, because a car pulls up in front of the house. I quickly go back in, go upstairs, and hide in the bathroom. I lie in the bath tub and pull the curtain. After a few minutes, someone comes in the bathroom in a hurry. I didn't see him, but I know it's a he, because he lifts the toilet seat. I pull the curtain and, aiming the gun at him, I shout.

"Drop whatever you're holding."

Our dear Maurice turn white and took his hands off the organ, raising them above his head.

"You can hold it for a little while longer. Look, you're peeing all around here."

He resumes the urination process while I get up from the tub.

"It's good to see you again. Isn't it that you missed me? Who are you with?"

"Alone."

"And when you're alone, you slam two doors in your car? Should we take it from the beginning? Come on, let's go downstairs!"

I tie his hands with the rope from the curtains and then we exit the bathroom. Downstairs, someone was rummaging in the kitchen.

"Hello, make me a coffee, Alina."

When she hears my voice she freezes. She turns around and smiles.

"Hello, what are you doing here?"

"I went out to buy some chips and I got lost. What are you doing here?"

"I finished the conference earlier and I thought I should come around here, because I haven't seen Maurice in a long time."

"Yes, it all makes sense. Yesterday you left from Romania to Greece. In the evening you already got to Lyon and today in Bordeaux. By my math, you should get to Beijing in about half an hour. Can you go there, please, and bring me some sushi?"

With my gun pointed at her, with Maurice tied up, I see myself obliged to do something in order to get out of this situation. I ask them to sit down on two chairs placed back to back. I untie their laces and tie them tightly by the legs of the metal chairs. With the rest of the rope, I tie them both by their hands, using the technique "tie them well, we have plenty of rope." Another uncomfortable position which allows them to move only their heads. I don't think that was necessary, but it gives me some additional safety.

"I apologize for leaving you two alone, but I'm a bit busy in the other room. If you need anything, shout!"

In the other room, I empty the luggage and start rummaging through it. Nothing in his, but when I open hers, two containers of hair spray make an infernal noise as they hit the floor. A tubby metallic sound. This is a bit strange.The fact that Alina doesn't really uses hair spray it makes me take one of the spray cans and go back in the kitchen, to them.

"From medic to hair stylist? You're throwing your money away on trash."

"It's none of your business what I do with my money."

"That's right, but what do we do when the money isn't yours?"

"You're wrong. I can justify any coin I put my hands on."

With a schnitzel hammer I blow the spray's head and I drop the content on the floor. Three rolls of money, head to head, fall out of it. A total of approximately twenty thousand euros.

"Where did you get those from?"

"From my investments in the country."

"What investments do you have that are so profitable?"

"It's none of your concern."

"On the contrary, madam, it is my business, and to a great extent."

"Miss to you."

"Maybe to others—for me you're a simple madam. You're both arrested for deprivation of freedom and murder."

"I'm glad you still have a sense of humor, Mr. Demetriad."

"I take life as a joke so it won't take me seriously, but unfortunately for you, now I'm serious."

"I believe you that you are obsessed with the case, but that's no reason to run around the world and arrest people everywhere."

"I wasn't even in a hurry to do this, and our discussion will lead nowhere. The French police will be here in a few moments."

"To do what?"

"To have a coffee and to take the evidence, if they have the time, of course."

"Evidence? Is there such thing?"

"Of course, my dear, of course."

"What, Marius' luggage? Yes, it was no kidnapping, it was just a vacation for him. He'll soon be back home."

"A rather expensive vacation, and paid for in a very dubious way. Moreover, not all his clothes are in his luggage. Some are in the backyard, in the ashes. They didn't have enough oxygen to burn completely."

"How do you know they're his? That's just stuff gathered from around the closets by Maurice when he cleaned up, and what couldn't be used anymore, we burnt. So what?"

"Maybe you're right. Maybe the boys armed with magnifying glasses and forceps from their laboratory at home will find some clues regarding the former owner of those clothes."

"This proves nothing!"

"The knife cuts for nothing, Alina. It will never be able to cut its own handle!"

"What do you mean by that?"

"You're clinging to any explanation in hope that you'll get away with it. No problem, the series of the bills used to pay the ransom were noted, and you'll have some explaining to do when they'll see those were in your bags."

"Yes, I admit I was wrong for not handing over the bag with money to the police when I found it."

"And how will you explain the murder?"

"What murder? I don't see any corpse."

"For now," I answer smiling while I pour a cup of coffee. "You don't think I'm going to start walking around here holding a stiff, do you? I bet a wagon full of giraffes that you didn't bother to leave any traces, knowing that the boy will rot there without anyone finding out!"

"Honestly, Dan, you're becoming paranoid. You're under the impression that you know everything, but you have no clue what you're talking about, and you're still hoping we'll admit to a murder we did not commit!"

"Mr. Demetriad to you."

"You're insane!" she shouts, exasperated by my attitude. She, unlike me, tries to worm things out of me, in case she will be forced to piece together a nice little story to cover her back. I wouldn't be surprised if she blamed it all on the poor foreigner, who was so foreign of this entire situation, dragged into all this dirt like a crocodile drags its prey back in the water to savor it.

An hour must have passed in which none of us said anything. I kept on refilling my cup of coffee, the only activity in the area. The two were getting rattled because numbness was already invading them, which made time pass a lot slower.

"When will the police get here?" Says Maurice.

"They're not really coming."

"You said they'll be here in a few moments," he replies with the voice of a kindergartner chastising his parents for not keeping their promise.

"I lied. It's very likely that I'll go to hell for this. I told them I'd call them when I had something concrete, and as your partner in torment says, I have nothing, so we'll wait until something comes up."

"You're insane," she repeats peacefully.

"Insane but not irresponsible. So, which one of you wants to start?"

"I already told you what I know. I'm willing to give a written statement.

"And will you also give us the approval to unearth you father so that we can recover the boy's body?"

As if we wouldn't have done it anyway, but I want to suggest to Alina that the story is over.

"Yes! Yes! Let's get this over with!"

"Superb!"

Our discussion ends here, because both of them tilt their heads, and in just a couple of minutes we can hear outside some cars decorated with lights and endowed with sirens pulling up. The French police showed up, just as they promised in case I contacted them. The two are arrested and taken to the station for questioning. I personally assist the discussion and then I request that Alina will be deported. Our homologous descendants of the king sun were nice, and while they handled all the necessary paperwork for deportation, I related the events, requesting that the child's body be sent back as soon as possible so that his parents could bury him without roommates. Thanks to the niceness mentioned above, we managed to take off to Romania the same day.

At the airport in Bucharest, authorities take Alina into custody and head straight for the jail. During the following few days I present all the proof and evidence I gathered.

Chapter IX
Or the chapter when,
Things become clear.
The first part of the last chapter

Maurice hadn't lied—the car was exactly where he said I'd find it, and the keys also. I get in and make a short inspection of the interior, then I leave for Craiova to meet with Marius' family.

"Cezar, my boy, what are you doing?"

"Fine, boss, monitoring Bogdan, but boss, I don't think I'll find out anything like this."

"Give up, Cezar. I solved the dilemma. I'm already on my way to Craiova."

"You did?! How did you do it, boss?!"

"I'll tell you everything about it when I get there. Did you manage to find the car?"

"No, boss, no sign of it. But we can declare that it was stolen in front of our hotel, and because we're police officers they'll buy it, and then we ca—"

"Calm down, I found it. It was walking the streets all by itself and sad."

"Uf, that's a relief."

"I'll talk to you when I get there. Go to Mihai and tell him I'll be there in a few hours."

He was happier hearing that I found the car than he was when he heard I found the boy. He's not a real policeman yet, but I'll see to that.

I get to Craiova and go directly to the Badea family, ignoring the late hour.

I go upstairs and head to the espressor, without saying any word besides a mumbled greeting, accompanied by their lethargic answers. They don't dare ask me anything, so I have to start after all.

"Looks like it all ends here. I found Marius."

"I think that … started Mihai, and then, pausing …

"Yes, he's dead."

"I kept on hoping this wouldn't happen."

"But he did it to himself."

"What do you mean by that?" Mihai intervened.

"Did he commit suicide?" completes Cristina.

"No, but he was behind the kidnapping the entire time."

Total shock on their faces, as if I had told them that half the planet collapsed into a sinkhole.

"How come?!"

"It was a setup. Marius was passionate about gambling. But since he lacked luck completely, he accumulated debt at casinos and tried to come up with the money. Initially, he borrowed from friends, but soon they refused to give him any more money. His first plan was to stage a burglary and steal money from you. Rudy was a collateral victim. They got rid of him to make sure he didn't cause any trouble.

But since you changed the alarm code, he gave up. Shortly thereafter, he came up with the idea of the kidnapping."

"But he couldn't have done this all by himself."

"Why not? You'd be amazed at the things people do to themselves, and this wouldn't be a problem if most of them didn't do it for pleasure. But since he trusted Alina, he thought that he could use her help, and through her he "contracted" several bodyguards who were loyal to her."

"Alina is involved?! And the guards? But you said they had no time to do this."

"Yes, she's involved. Now she is arrested and will stand trial."

"And where is Marius?"

"I already discussed with the French police, they'll send him to the country, he will be autopsied here, and then he'll arrive home."

The atmosphere was sad, blank, clogged. Cristina was crying in her hands, sitting on the armchair. Mihai was walking around the room, trying to understand exactly what was going on. From his look, I understood that only now had he realized he had a child. It's a paradox, finding out you have a child only when he dies, not when he's born. Their pain affects Cezar, who's barely holding back his tears. Me? For me it was just another solved case. Nothing special. I must admit that in the beginning, I was also impressed, but when you get to see so many victims and grieving families, you become immune.

"We will be leaving. I hope we'll meet again!" I say while I reach out to Mihai.

"Yes, thank you for your help. I hope we'll meet again too!"

Cristina mumbles a greeting through her tears and we leave from the Badea house for the last time. At least for the moment. We head back to the hotel, where I hope I'll catch a few hours of sleep, and then we'll leave toward who knows where. Cezar is quiet and seems to be very upset. I sit down on the armchair and light up a cigar.

"Why are you disappointed, Cezar?"

"Because, you see, it's my first case and I was hoping we wouldn't blow it."

"You're wrong. Who says we blew it?"

"Well the boy is dead."

"He was just part of the whole. Your success is always in other's failure. We were contacted, and the investigation led us to solve the case. Stop thinking about it and get to sleep. Tomorrow I'll explain the reasoning that led to finding the guilty persons."

"Yes, good night, boss!"

Part two of the last chapter

I slept like the *Titanic* at the bottom of the ocean. My brain understands that it's time to focus its attention on storing the useful information we gathered in this current investigation and fully take advantage of this. We wake up almost at noon, and that is because the people from the hotel were nice enough to wake us up so we can leave. We stop in Pitesti at an inn, and with a coffee in front of me. I arm myself with patience to detail for the kid, who has armed himself with a notebook and a pen, exactly what happened.

"Boss, how did you realize that Marius is involved?"

"I only suspected. I found out from Ingrid, and then from Maurice, that the boy didn't seem at all constrained or forced. If you add the money problems and, implicitly, the "robbery" that didn't take place, you can already ask yourself serious questions. But this situation seemed too complicated to be his idea. He could have done things a lot more simply, for example, not contacting me in this case."

"And why exactly you?"

"Because I was the target. He tried to chew more than he could swallow."

"Why were you the target, boss?"

"One of the days, Mihai met someone who was panicked that Paraschiv was locked up, and from what he had hold him, I realized that it was Cap-de-Tun who had framed the suicide of those two sneak-thieves.[11] Only then I realized why me. The guy, revenger and stubborn, was keen on giving me a lesson, and it was impossible for him to find someone who would target me, regardless of how much he offered for this service. Trifon spoke to us about the same character and about the fact that Marius owed him, so he tried to take advantage of the boy, who had no obvious connections to the world of crime so far. It's possible that he proposed to wipe out his entire debt in return for bringing me here for the investigation."

"And how did Paraschiv know about the kidnapping?"

"Don't you think that Marius would have told him? He needed to come up with the money to pay his debt and gave the incarcerated details regarding the way he would get them."

"You're right. How about Bogdan?"

---

11 "Cap-de-Tun" – Cannon-Head.

"Bogdan, except for the episode with Rudy, was not involved in any way. His mistake was sticking around Alina for too long. She kept pushing him forward, to keep us off the scent, so that they had the time to come up with a concrete plan against me."

"I still can't figure out how you figured out that the transactions were made from Mrs. Ingrid's account."

"It was necessary that someone spilled my coffee."

"Meaning?"

"I mean the guy spilled my coffee, and the next he paid by card. A personalized card that didn't look at all as a payment instrument; this is how I remembered seeing in Alina's wallet what I thought then was a business card of Ingrid. Small fees for international transactions, blocked personal accounts, or any other pretext would have worked to convince her to borrow her card. This would have been no problem for Alina. A smart move, because she thought I would verify the transactions she made, and so she would escape from an inconvenient situation in which I was monitoring her."

"And when did you notice the 'business card'?"

"When I went at Alina's house. That was also the moment they chose to stop my heart one way or another."

"Maybe she just wanted to fool around."

"That was exactly what I initially thought, but it had all been planned carefully. She was expecting that I would search for clues, and to take my mind off the thought of suspecting her because of her trip to Greece, she had "thrown" a diploma on the table indicating her participation at a medical conference. A pretty good fake. Only a professional would have realized that one stamp is tridimensional and the emblem of the Hellenic state had been cut with a professional editing software, but by a beginner. And the night when she left, I tried to contact her only minutes after she had spoken to Mihai. Her phone seemed to be off. But actually, and she didn't answer because the prefix for Greece was not the correct one. Even her reaction as she found out that I was staying in Craiova to handle the investigation for the club assassination gave her away. To make sure, I suggested that the police be notified about the kidnapping, and she bought it, saying that it was better that they didn't."

"And the charts with the guards from the clubs were also forged, right?"

"No, she had no access to those charts, and anyway, she wasn't interested in this aspect. The charts from Arcade never made it to me, because Mihai didn't interfere at all in what she was doing there. This is also the reason she got involved in the kidnapping. She owed Badea a nice amount of money, and since the club wasn't going as she had hoped, she needed to find the money from another source. So, on the first day, Alina left with Marius at Bucharest and took him to her cousin, Ingrid. There they took the picture with the newspaper, and then she returned alone the following day. During this time, he left with the other four persons, three bodyguards from the club and a friend of hers, French, whom she had met during her extended vacation in France. He was supposed to handle everything while she was missing, because she didn't trust the boy and even less the accompanying buffalos."

"And where did they go?"

"At her parents' house. They even lived there for a while. Meanwhile, they gave me the newspaper, since Alina saw that I was becoming rather uncomfortable. And they dropped everything to see if I would or would not continue the investigation, and when they saw I was not involved anymore, they called to demand the money."

"And why didn't Marius come home after they took the money?"

"I don't think he wanted to come back. This meant he needed to pay his debts in full, since they didn't manage to get rid of me. So they decided to go to France, to Alina's friend, Maurice. They stayed in a rented house, paid by Alina with money she took from the club, because they were expecting that the bills would be registered, so they kept them hidden. There, something happened, and they fought. I realized it was about the money. I can't see any other reason for dispute. Then the girl applied a powerful hit on his head with a vase. This fight made her think of the possibility of excluding him from the equation. The story was also confirmed by her during the interrogation, saying that he no longer wanted her half the money, as they initially established, but only ten percent, from which she had to pay her 'aids' but no longer had enough money to restitute the entire amount to Badea and bring round the club."

"That's when he died?"

"No, that's when she decided with Maurice, who had to return to Bordeaux for his father's funeral, to get him there and get rid of him."

"But how did they transport him? Didn't anyone see them?"

"They did, there were three persons in a car, one of them sleeping. They drugged him until he couldn't even remember his name. You can imagine that he was high and was fishing stars with his fingertips. He wasn't interested that he was heading to a mine field. And only in Bordeaux they killed him."

"Did she say how?"

"No, the autopsy will take place in Bucharest, and then we'll learn exactly what happened. I think that in a moment of panic she stabbed him and he died, because they tried to burn some clothes soaked in blood. Maurice asked that he be left alone with his father, and they put Marius' body under that of Mr. Villain. I didn't have enough time to inspect the house, but I did find in the bath tub, around the drain, traces of blood that they didn't succeed in removing. Definitely the police will find others around the house. I also found the money. She had carried it across the border for her second 'conference' in Greece. She had hidden it in hairspray canisters. The police took them as evidence, but at some point they'll give it back."

"And how did you find the body?"

"When I went to the cemetery I learned that Maurice's father didn't have a well-developed physique, but next to the grave I saw the footprints of those who helped lowering the coffin, because they did it manually. And the footprints were very deep in comparison to those of the other participants. The coffin was two times heavier."

"Maybe if we managed to talk with his boxing coach we could have managed to find them sooner and to avoid the tragic ending."

"This wasn't possible, Cezar. I had to use the scheme with the basketball in order to get some details, because people avoid getting involved or giving information when it comes to Mihai, regardless of how useful it is."

"Tricky situation."

"You'll get used to it—you'll see."

"Used to what, boss?"

"Such moments. The important thing is that you don't lose your focus, not even for a second, from beginning to end. Don't worry—this will never happen to you!"

"That's right, never! I'll always stay concentrated."

"Like packed soup, kid, packed soup!"

"Yes, like packed soup! What do you mean, boss, like packed soup?"

"I mean powder! You still have a lot to learn. Don't let it go to your head that you're a policeman already!"

This was for him not to forget who's boss. The excess of severity generates hate, but the excess of indulgence weakens authority! The vacation will be mine only. I'm being selfish, but he still didn't deserve a vacation, so starting from tomorrow, he'll start doing paperwork.

"Kid, isn't it the case that you knew this entire time that it wasn't Bogdan, but you wanted to keep me in suspense?"

"It didn't even run through my head, boss."

"That's why I like you, Cezar." I smile at him.

We get up from the table and go down the road, which was decorated, besides the intense green of fields, with a sun that was streaming down our faces, letting us know that he was leaving too, for now, because the following day will arrive only to destroy another morning for me. And this is how tomorrow, today becomes yesterday.

THE END

If you enjoyed it then why stop here? In the second book, I struggle to recover the two weeks of my life that were stolen from me. This is how it all began...

Let there be time!
Chapter Alpha
Or the Genesis

I open only one eye, in case there's someone lurking to stick a finger deep in it, and stare at the ceiling. Nothing. I move all my limbs without looking. Stupid gesture, because if they weren't where they were supposed to be, my brain would be capable of lying to me that I'm whole, so that I won't panic. I dare to open my other eye for a full view. Fortunately, I'm whole. Unfortunately, I'm like a master station, with tubing and cable sticking out from every part of my body. The room in spacious enough, but the white of the walls make it look even bigger. I count a total of eight beds, including my own. We're all connected to some big white boxes that look like they sonars of German submarines. In the bed on my left I see a middle-aged woman, hanging between life and death. I think the second option fits her better. Her blank look staring right at me stops dead and the beeping white box yells that the lady has left this world. Her eyes are trying to reproach me with the cruelty of life. "Dear madam, with all due respect, you should've thought when you were born that you'll also die. Don't come now complaining to me that you ran out of days. We're born alone, we die alone, and during the whole time in between, we're on our own," I think toward her. I'm too weak to articulate words. Meanwhile, an army of nurses bounce into the room and struggle to resuscitate her. I slowly turn my head to the left, where a man also closes his business with life.

I think he had some arrears to pay, and he had to remain in a coma until he solved them. I wasn't disturbed by his presence, but the little box was making a rare and bold sound, out of step with the breaths of air he struggled to take. I scan the ward and notice that I'm the only one in it who's almost alive. I resign myself to the thought that I'm still under the effect of the anesthetic, which loses strength, and the pain starts to reappear, together with images of the previous day. They are too many and they come to my mind in a chaotic manner. I avoid using my brain for now. It might malfunction and I'm sure I'm going to need it later. I feel a burn in my stomach—that's probably where I received my share of lead. I still can't coordinate my moves, but I can speak. So I prepare to demand an explanation and shout, "I want a coffee!"

In return, I receive a large cup of indifference from the angels in white from the ward. I think I just thought out loud, as my voice still doesn't work. I try again,—unsuccessfully, of course—and I fall asleep.

Again, light. Again, pains, again, angels in white. Only this time they're all standing around my bed. I have probably crossed to the other side of the barricade, because I also see Saint Peter among them.

"Good morning, Mr. Demetriad!"

"Good morning!" I answer to the gatekeeper from the entrance to Paradise.

"I'm the doctor who operated on you. Dumitrache is my name. How are you feeling?"

"Whole. I'm waiting for a second opinion to confirm that."

"Indeed, you're whole, at least on the outside. On the interior we had to fix some things to make sure you'll be fine."

"That's a relief. And what exactly needed repairs on the inside?"

"One of the bullets has gone through the abdomen and fixed in the duodenum, this being the most dangerous of all. We had to surgically intervene so we could close the wound, and of course to perform a lavage, because almost the entire content of your stomach spilled. The other two bullets did not affect any vital organs and will leave marks only on the surface. Both hit the right side."

"Should I understand that all the coffee I had before the accident was spilled? No wonder I'm so sleepy. Could I have a large cup of coffee right now? And I'll need my clothes and a lighter, because that's where I was headed."

"Not really. You'll remain under observation at Intensive Care Unit for a few days, during which time you'll not consume any kind of food or fluids."

"Already I feel like home! And still, could I have a cup of coffee?"

"No way. Just perfusions."

"Perfect! I'd like two perfusions of coffee and one with fries flavour."

He looks just like a waiter writing down my order. After he scribbles in his report, he turns around and leaves to attend to the next goner in the area, leaving me in the care of the gentle angels. After they start fueling me with glucose, they disperse through the ward, and only one staying by my side. It was love at first sight. The morphine amplified the feeling, and for a second I really thought we are alone on an empty beach. Her blond hair is fighting with the wind, like the Vikings fighting the storms on the sea, and her eyes are smiling, looking at me. A smile took shape on her lips, and a shy dimple made its way onto one of her cheeks. She approaches me and whispers, gifting me a urinal.

"Try to urinate. Your bladder is full. If you can't do it, we'll have to insert a catheter."

"That's also a way of getting me naked, but know that I don't go all the way on the first date."

I take the urinal and put it in a comfortable position, waiting for the flow. She is now standing near another bed, regulating an old man's IV. I'm not a shy guy—when I have to go, I go—but now it was a little different. Her image, in her white robe, through which I could see her shape, long and soft legs, the thought that I lie here like a wreck, but also the idea of a catheter, makes it hard to concentrate on urinating. Nothing, no sign. The thought of an object crammed in my organ is already making me panic, so I clench my teeth, close my eyes, and imagine rivers, seas, oceans, sinks with broken faucets, waterfalls—anything containing $H2O$. The effect is marvelous—I'm almost there, I can feel it! I feel myself dripping into the urinal. In the end, proud of myself, I smile to her and show her the urinal from under the blanket. She smiles back and takes from a drawer a small package containing various objects, among which is a hose. I look at the urinal. It was empty. It all happened in my head. To hell with it, I'm going to be probed! There followed a mixture of pain, curiosity, pleasure, and a grimace. And then, sleep.

SubchapterA.
Regenesis

I already feel better. I've been moved to a side room, next to a suffering old man who is more cheerful than me. The room is small—there are two beds and a small table between them. The walls are an immaculate white, and here and there one can see a hose, a button, and various strange items necessary for resuscitation. Too much white, and my eyes hurt. I feel some fresh mountain air coming through my nose. I perform a short verification: two tubes in my belly, one in my nose over which there's an oxygen mask, another one in my organ, and an IV in each hand. Yes, I'm complete. Now I could really use a retrospective of yesterday. Maybe I'll realize who and why.

Subchapter B.
Bang Bang. How stupid.

It's morning, and I head to the corner coffee shop. This is unusual, because I'm never in the mood to leave the house in the morning. I have to meet with Bernard. Bernie is a French informant who made our job easier in many different situations. He's a nice, monotonous polyglot, perfect for not raising suspicions. I see him making his way through cars and cursing. His Romanian is so funny, with an accent on his Rs that makes it impossible to get upset with whatever he says. He has nothing out of the ordinary, short hair and brown eyes, symmetrical features, without any kind of accessory that would draw attention on him. You can tell he's experienced on the job. He comes straight toward me and sits down at the table nervous, cursing between his teeth.

"*Merde*! These guys took driving lessons with monkeys, that's why they chatter so loud ?"

"Bernie, that round green one on the traffic light was for them. Yours was that little man with his feet spread and unlit."

"That's just an excuse."

"And a universally valid law. When incurable diseases appeared the planet had a negative growth so they invented traffic lights to keep a balance. With less car accidents, we had again a positive growth. Easy as that.

"Yes, whatever. I won't forgive them!"

"Any news?"

"My next door neighbor won the Lotto."

"A lot?"

"Not exactly the jackpot, but enough to afford not to work for a few good years."

"I understand. And when's he going to collect the money?"

"It still must be decided when and where.For now, since it's a relatively large amount. Things are being established very carefully, and they won't involve anyone unless it's absolutely necessary."

"Do you know where he purchased his ticket from?"

"Yes, you have all details in a file that will be delivered to you today by courier. To make it short I could say that—"

"We should get away from here."

"Are you thinking about that couple standing near the crosswalk?"

"Yes, they've been sitting there for a good few minutes, waiting to cross, and it seems they're interested in everything other than the color of the traffic light."

"I know. I saw them earlier—that's why I tried to create a little fuss. I hoped they'd get it and leave."

"I'll look over the file when I'll receive it and we'll meet at Excalibur after nine. I'll have a wine. Red if possible."

"*Oui.* I'll see you tonight. *Au revoir!*"

He gets up and disappears into the crowd right away. The two are still there. Could it be that I'm the one who's being watched? I mean, I wouldn't be surprised—it's not the first time someone tried something on me, but never that obvious. I'd either wake up with them at my doorstep, with bats matching their shoes, or be ambushed some other way. But surveillance?"

I peacefully finish my coffee and head home. I'm not going to invite them over, as I haven't cleaned up in some time, so I walk them around the park for a while. The rotating camera on my phone allows me to subtly look behind me. They're already becoming too obvious—they're just a few meters away from me and watching me intently. I take them to a highly populated area to make sure they won't try anything, and I turn around directly toward them. The moment they both stop and stare at me, I take advantage of the moment, startling them by heading right toward us them.

"Problems?"

"What?"

"I was wondering if you have any problems. I see that you're very agitated.

"No, sir. What's gotten into you?"

"This was my second question, but since you got ahead of me, I'll explain it for you. After the twenty minutes you spent near the crosswalk, during which you were staring at me, you started walking behind me, and from all the alleys possible in this park you chose exactly the random route I circled. I can tell you don't do this very often. You thought you looked enough like a couple so you won't be noticed, but you're holding each other like you're grounded, and you haven't exchanged one word the whole time. Plus, you both wear wedding rings, but different models. No offence, but you're too weak to be criminals, so let's not hide anymore. Let's chat."

"We're—"

"Don't even bother lying to me. We're wasting time."

"We're reporters. We want to write an article about private investigators and their modus operandi, and we thought you'd be a good subject."

"I wanted to be a guinea pig for such a long time. Do you think it's enough that I'm alive, or do I have to do a magic trick to make it interesting? Look for another subject. I really don't need any additional stress."

I quietly leave for my home. I think I'm already becoming paranoid. Next I'll start suspecting the mailman of putting bombs in my envelopes. I get home a little after lunchtime, and only a few minutes later arrives the courier, who's delivering a large and clangorous box. I open it and inside I find a stuffed toy, some local newspapers, and a box of chocolate. How nice of him. I find the necessary information inside the chocolate box. There are a few addresses from different countries where the target does his business. The lotto prize is nothing more than a major transaction, planned a very long time ago, and very ingenious. He's selling people as someone in the market sells cucumbers. We know that he keeps them on the move, spending just a couple of days in a location before moving on and when they decide to do the transaction, he'll bring them all together. Human trafficking is blooming, and since some of our fellow countrymen have the brain of a squid, they're very easy to allure. The case was thrown on my table by the guys from Missing Persons, who seem to have very little control over things. It didn't bother me one bit, as I get a risk increment. This in case anyone has doubts whether I do it for reasons of humanity or for money. A warm shower completely drowses me and makes me lose any mood for going out. But I have to, so I slowly leave for Excalibur. The darkness outside breaks a few meters above ground, where the light poles scatters the darkness and turns it into a pale light. It's crowded inside—all the better, so no one will notice us. I see Bernie and I observe as he's staying at the table, absently smoking a cigar. I turn around and I get out. It's really serious. On the table he had a bottle of white wine, which, in our language, means that the meeting has been canceled for various reasons. And the reason is serious enough, since after only ten minutes at the table he had smoked not less than five cigars and was in the process of burning one more. I cross the street and I also light up a cigar. I see him coming out, with four other persons following him. A car pulls in front of him, and in a fraction of a second he disappears inside, pushed by one of the followers, who continue walking freely. I start walking in the same direction, across the street from them, at a good pace. I take out my phone and I call Cezar just as a courtesy.

"Hi, are you sleeping?"

"No, just browsing through the TV channels. I'm sick and tired, boss. I can't wait to take off my plaster so I can leave the house."

"Are you hurrying somewhere? We don't have much work, anyway. Take full advantage of this break. You only have one week, and you'll start recovering. Then you'll be able to run a marathon."

"I hope so. I really run out of patience. How's it going for you? Any work?"

"Fortunately, no. I'll call you in a few minutes. I have something to do."

I suddenly interrupt the discussion because the happy guys are all facing me, holding something in their hands. I'm sure they're not lollipops, and by the bang they make I see they are guns. A few rounds in my direction and the image becomes blurry. I manage to dial the emergency number we have in case of, obviously, emergencies, and I look for a spot where I can lie down and rest for a while. I think the pool of blood forming under me is good enough. I collapse.

Chapter 2
And off I went...

Subchapter A
"Somebody owes me!"

Time. Yes, time owes me. While I'm enjoying the silence in my room, Cezar comes in. This would only be possible if yesterday wasn't yesterday. It's yesterday only for me, because someone stole some days from my calendar. I hope they didn't take too many.

"What date is today?"

"Hey, boss, look, I can walk. I still limp a bit, but it's okay. The important thing is that I can walk!"

"Lazarus, I'm glad you got up, but I also want to know if I'm Jesus, resurrected after only three days, or if I slacked more. What date is today?"

"It's April sixteenth."

"Superb, I was a vegetable for two weeks. I want a piece of paper and a pen. I'm filing a complaint."

"Against who?"

"Cronos. Isn't he the guy with the clock?"

"Who?"

"Never mind."

Meanwhile I press my hand on the button over me, and in record time a nurse shows up. It's the same one who handled the implementation of the catheter. I will never forget her. I don't know if morphine is doing this, or she really looks so good.

"Hello, is anything wrong?"

"Hello, no, nothing out of the ordinary."

"What?"

"We were talking about my coma and whether it's not out of the ordinary to lay senseless for two weeks on occasion."

"You should be happy that you're alive, rather than complaining that you were in a coma."

"Thank you. I'm alive minus two weeks. I have an incomplete life now. What happened, in fact?"

"After the surgery there were minor complications, and your body reacted differently than expected, so we had to induce a coma. Your body was fighting against itself."

"Is this the academic version of the fact that you left a clipper and two bolt nuts inside me?"

"No, it's the short version of the fact that …"

I have already lost interest in the details. If today is the sixteenth, it means that the transaction already took place. And besides the persons who are already transacted, we have one French informant less. And above this, a good friend as well!

"I need your phone number."

"What for? "

Because I no longer have Internet at my house. Clearly I was late in paying the bill, and I could really use a medical dictionary."

"Very funny, but it's not possible."

"For now."

"For now, I'm going to leave. If you no longer need anything, I'll see you in the morning."

"Should I understand you're asking me out? Are you taking me out for an IV?" I match this line with a wide smile between the tubes, and she answers shyly. I turn to Cezar in hopes of finding out anything. Small chance of that. During that period he was confined in his bed because of his broken leg, and he also didn't know anything about the activity I was involved in. And he won't find anything out. It's for his own protection that he's not involved. Things have already gained momentum.

"Is there any lead on those who shot me?"

"Not for now. They were expecting you to recover so that they could talk to you."

"Great, things are already sorted out. I remember them perfectly. There were four guys in black leather jackets who appeared, and suddenly they started shooting. I think now I could use a trip to the world of dreams. I'll wait for you tomorrow morning to discuss more."

"Fine, I'll go back to the station. Maybe I'll manage to find out something."

The door of the room closes behind him, and in a few minutes my eyes are closed as well.

Subchapter B
Here's trouble ...

I understand that he got terribly bored during the whole period when he had to stay confined in bed, but that doesn't excuse him for being at my bedside at only 7 a.m.

"Good morning, boss!"

"Maybe for you. For me it's still night."

"I searched yesterday through the files of the previous investigations. You know, those with maximum risk."

"Yes, I have them all in my head, and believe me, you solved nothing. I'm on the black list of too many persons, so you won't find anything useful. And there is still the possibility that it was only an accident."

I know it was no accident, and I also know that the mission is safe as long as Cezar handles the investigation. I'll send him through corn fields to bring me barley, so I'll peacefully mind my own business.

"However, you could ask Paraschiv some questions. I don't think he forgave me for his idiocy, and it wouldn't be the first time he tried something. Probably now he's just lost his mind. Keep me updating regarding the situation."

"I'll go today to talk to him, and I'll check the case again. Maybe I missed something."

He gets up to leave, and at the door he intersects with the nurse who was coming to deliver breakfast for me.

"Good morning. Did you sleep well?"

"Yes, I really needed some rest after how much I ran these last couple of weeks on the fields of unconsciousness."

"But what happened to you?"

"Nothing. It seems I fell asleep with a bottle of diazepam in my mouth, and it dissolved slowly enough to keep me asleep for a long time."

"It happens."

Her eyes fixed on the empty perfusion bags, and then she took from the tray, which was already in the room, a few bags of glucose and saline solution to change them and to add the magic liquor to my installation.

"I think you should stop."

She stopped. I don't think that my courteous look had any success, but my Glock pointed at her did. The toy was brought by Cezar earlier, as I thought I should have a firecracker at hand in case I wasn't satisfied by the room service. With my other hand I push the magic button and through the door enters Stefania, the nurse I was expecting to come and change my perfusions. It wasn't at all difficult to realize that I have in front of me another attempted murder. The way she changed the perfusion bags, the syringes she already had prepared in her pocket, and if she had worked the last couple of weeks in the hospital, she surely knew about me, the cop who's lying in a coma . If I was wrong, there wasn't too much damage, just a scared nurse who would need to take some leave to clear her head. The door opens wide, and a scream—I must admit, a very sexy one—distracts my attention. Stefania stands in the door, with her hands over her mouth and with eyes the size of melons. She was cute, even like that. In a way, I feel bad in front of her. Even during our first meetings she caught me with another woman.

"Call hospital security, please. This miss here wanted to ruin our date." The next second, she disappeared, and I could hear her footsteps running down the hallway.

"Who sent you here?"

She was leaning against the table and was staring blank.

"Did you know I can do permanent but not lethal damage with a bullet in one of your limbs and say afterwards it was self-defense? However, it would be easier if you spoke."

The party is broken up by the happy guys from security. This girl moves so fast! Interesting reaction of theirs, though. They both pointed their guns at me.

"Put your weapon down!"

"If you intend to shoot, aim for the already existing holes. I don't want to damage the packaging more that in already is. Chief Quaestor

Dan Demetriad. Strangely, the miss standing next to me is more dangerous than I am."

"What happened here?"

"I'm under the impression that she has mixed up my medications. Could you check, however."

Both of them grabbed her by the arms and removed her from the room, also taking the syringes to check them for poisons.

"I apologize for the situation. I light up rather quickly when it's my life at stake."

"Incredible. Who could do such a thing?"

"It's possible it's the milkman. A few days ago I returned a couple of unwashed bottles, and this might have irritated him. Do you think you could bring my perfusions and a double dose of morphine? I believe I've disturbed my fissures."

"Yes, right away."

After she came back we had a small chat. Of course, without crossing the limit of the patient-doctor relationship. The situation was fine for me. I really felt the need to socialize in a banal manner, without getting lost in thoughts and problems. And as days were passing by, hoses were coming out of me, and just a week later I was ready to stand and eat biscuits. The security ensured by the police satisfied my need for socialization, and still I couldn't completely escape my thoughts. The killer girl told everything to the police. Stupid and useless. Someone approached her the day prior to the attempt, under the pretext that they were planning a surprise party and that she should administer a strong sleeping agent so that my "friends" could decorate my room with balloons and confetti. She bought the whole story, and she was this close to giving me a portion of cyanide, which was also confirmed by the laboratory, after which she would decorate my room with candles and crowns. Things weren't safe anymore in the country. The collaborators of the human trafficking network were already onto me, and the bad part is that I didn't have the slightest clue who they were. The day I was so eagerly expecting came, and Cezar was waiting for me in front of the hospital, ready to take me home.

I didn't pay any attention to him at all. My mind was scattered in all cardinal points, in a desperate attempt to find solutions. We get to the apartment and, exactly as I expected, the maid I don't have exaggerated with the cleaning.

"At least they didn't take my collection of beer can rings," I tell Cezar, smiling ironically.

"It's a total mess!"

"Good observation, Cezar. Did you figure it out yourself, or did you suspect that because of the furniture lying everywhere and the papers thrown on the floor among everything else? It's not safe for me to stay here. Help me get some things, and we're going to the station until I can find a solution."

Of course, the file was missing. But also many other documents, which transformed me into the easiest target possible. I get my lucky ashtray and cup and I head for the station with Cezar, who wouldn't stop asking questions and making assumptions. Of course, his investigation was stagnating—the barley was nowhere to be found. I'm still not completely recovered, and I get tired rather quickly, so the trip to the office completely exhausts me. Moreover, I'm not allowed to drink coffee anymore, so I pour milk over it so that my brain doesn't realize I still drink it. If they didn't manage to kill me, I'll do it, slowly and with ritual.

The continuation will come as soon as possible, and you will definitely find it in the same place where you found the first volume.